QUEEN OF KLUTZ

Sibby Series Book 1

SAMANTHA GARMAN

Tabula Rasa Publishing

For those who have ever worked in the customer service industry, I salute you.

Disclaimer

No fictional people were offended during the writing of this book.

Chapter 1

Trippa: [tree-pah]
    1. Tripe. Stomach of a pig, cow, or sheep.
    2. Uhm. Ew.

    I blinked, wondering if I looked like that cartoon owl from the old Tootsie Pop commercial. "Say again?"

    My boss leaned back in his office chair and said, "I've got to let you go, Sibby. Hate to do it, and it's not personal. It's the economic climate. Things have changed; things have slowed down. So we have to downsize."

    Economic climate?

    I thought only uppity financial spokespeople used that

phrase. "Ed, please don't do this to me," I pleaded. "I'm good at editing textbook copy. I know how to format e-books. I can do more, really. I'll even work for less!" I sounded desperate, and at that moment, I really didn't like myself.

But Mama had to eat. And pay rent. And fly to Boca to visit her grandparents. They played shuffleboard. What the hell was shuffleboard, anyway?

"I'm sorry. I know you're really good at your job."

"Then why is this happening? Is it how I dress? I can start wearing boxy suits and clunky heels if that helps."

I looked down at my scuffed, grey Converse sneakers and skinny-leg jeans. I didn't have to deal with customers face to face, so it never really mattered how I looked. Or so I had thought.

"I'm not letting you go because of how you dress. There's nothing wrong with dressing like a college student."

"Hipster," I muttered, gently pushing up my jet-black Spencer Tracy frames.

"I'm gonna miss your sense of humor," he said, shaking his head like he deeply regretted firing me. "You can use me as a reference."

"Reference? You made me put on real pants and trek from Brooklyn so you could *fire me?* On a *Monday?* Who does that?"

"I needed the weekend—I was trying to think of a way to keep you on, but I just can't. And I didn't want to fire you over the phone. I owe you that much, at least."

"Oh—thanks? I guess begging at this point is just a little pathetic?"

He gave me a sad smile. It only made me feel more inadequate.

I stood, feeling all the blood rush from my head.

Passing out would sink what little pride I had left. "Guess that's it then, huh?"

"Take care, Sibby."

I snatched my messenger bag off the back of the chair and promptly dropped it, spilling its contents all over the floor.

Awkward.

I stepped outside to a hot, humid, overcast July afternoon and started sweating immediately.

Sexy.

Okay, it was time to go home and regroup. I walked to the subway, found a seat on a Brooklyn bound train, and marveled at the lack of people. During rush hour it was nearly impossible to get a seat, and I was almost always forced to stand with my face in someone's armpit.

Being short sucked.

When I got off the train, I tried to call my boyfriend Matt. No answer. That wasn't shocking since I knew he kept his cell in a desk drawer so he could get work done without being distracted. Oh well, he'd be home around six. I'd vent about my day and then we'd get tanked. In the meantime, I'd eat a lot of ice cream. Maybe I'd stop by a bakery and get a box of donuts. Eating my emotions sounded pretty good.

I trudged up the fourth-floor walk-up, mentally

whining like I was climbing Mount Everest. I sank my key into the lock, walked into the one-bedroom apartment, and tripped over Matt's shoes.

Dress shoes.

Shoes he only wore to work.

So why were they by the door?

I heard a deep, masculine chuckle.

Approaching the bedroom, I heard the laugh again.

I pushed the door open—

And saw my live-in boyfriend of two years in bed with another man.

Oh. My. God.

"Sibby!" Matt exclaimed, scrambling to cover himself. "What are you doing home?"

I glared. "Wrong question." He was naked from the waist up, showing off his impeccably muscled chest. He was hairless and tan. He hadn't always looked like that. I should've known something was up when he started drinking protein shakes and working out all the time.

His companion unfolded himself and got out of bed, grabbing his boxers from the floor. Before he put them on, I got a full view of his package.

Yowsa!

I'd been clobbered once already, what with getting fired. Then I walked in on my boyfriend cheating on me. With a dude.

Worst. Day. Ever.

I slid my phone out of my pocket and called my bestest friend in the world, Annie.

"What up?" she answered.

"Can you meet me?"

"Meet you? It's two in the afternoon. Aren't you at work?"

"No."

There was a pause. "Where are you?"

"At a bar on the Upper East Side."

"You're drinking before sunset. In my neighborhood? You never come up here."

"It's bad, Annie."

"How bad."

"Bad bad."

She sighed. "Give me fifteen minutes. I'm cleaning up lunch at Heather's and then I'm all yours."

"I'm at O'Brien's." I hung up. "Another tequila pineapple please," I said to the bartender.

"You shouldn't drink alone," he said. He was cute, with an Irish lilt.

"I'm waiting on a friend."

He peered at me with sympathetic eyes. "You wanna talk about it?"

"Nope."

Bartenders tended to be cheaper than psychologists, but far less effective.

5

Twenty minutes later, Annie walked in. She had an enviable rack and a blond, tamable mane. She loved sports and didn't get attached to guys. Our friendship went back to freshman year in college and we were intensely loyal to each other.

Without saying a word, she plopped down a bar of dark chocolate in front of me.

The good, organic, 80% cacao kind.

"You get me," I stated.

"What number are you on?" she asked, hanging her purse on a hook underneath the bar.

"I don't know, ask him," I said, gesturing to the bartender with my drink, liquid sloshing over the rim of the glass.

"Vodka tonic please. And what number is she on?"

"Three." Only it sounded like he said *tree* because of his accent.

"Three?" Annie raised her eyebrows. "How long have you been here?"

"An hour," the bartender answered for me, grabbing a highball glass and filling it with ice.

"So, what brought about this day-drinking?" Annie asked.

"It hits in threes," I said. "Or *trees*." I couldn't do an Irish lilt to save my life.

"What does?"

"Tragedies."

"Oh, boy. Start with the first one," Annie stated, taking a sip of her drink.

"Well, I got fired this morning."

"What? Why? You're good at your boring job!"

"Hey," I protested. She looked at me and my shoulders sagged. "Yeah, all right, but it was still a job—my job. I'm a fan of money. It pays for things like, you know, rent and food."

"And tequila pineapples."

"Exactly. Then I go home and catch Matt in bread with someone."

"Bread?" Annie asked.

"I think she means *bed*," the bartender offered.

"I got that, thanks," Annie said sarcastically.

"Just trying to help," he said.

"Can you not listen?" I demanded of him. "You're hot and Irish, but I really, really don't need a stranger witnessing my drunken misery."

"I respect that," he said stepping away to the other end of the bar.

"What did she look like?" Annie asked.

"Who?"

"The woman you found Matt in bed with."

"I never said it was a woman."

Annie's eyes opened wide. "No."

"Yes."

"Matt's gay?" both Annie and the bartender said in unison.

"Little bit." I looked at the bartender. "I told you not to listen!"

He shrugged, but said nothing.

"Holy shit on a stick!" Annie said.

I rested my head on the wooden bar. "I refuse to go home tonight. I can't face Matt."

"You can stay with me. We could be roomies!"

"You live in a teeny tiny box, and your bed is lofted. There's barely enough room for *you.*"

"Okay, so you'll have to go home. Eventually. But tonight you can crash on my futon."

"One less thing to worry about. What am I gonna do about the other stuff?" I moaned.

"About Matt and the job?"

I lifted my head and nodded.

"Don't do anything for the time being. We're going out tonight."

"I don't want to go out."

"You're already out."

"Oh, yeah. True."

"Matt is a total wanker."

"Thank you for that," I murmured.

"I'll take you to all my favorite bars. We'll play pool and flirt with guys who wear polos."

"I hate the Upper East Side."

"This is my terrain, Sib. I got ya covered. Now, drink up so we can get to our next stop."

"What's our next stop?"

"Falafel. You need fuel if you're going to go out like I go out."

"I can't party like you. I'm not frozen at nineteen."

"That might be the nicest thing you've ever said to me," she teased. "Now drink up."

I munched on a falafel that was as big as my face, my tongue numb from the spicy sauce. "I think I'm feeling a bit better about Matt," I said.

Annie raised her eyebrows. "It's been like ten minutes. And you found out you were a beard for two years—that doesn't just go away because you eat a falafel."

"There's something I've been keeping from you."

"Go on…"

"Put your pita down first," I said. "I don't want you to drop it in shock."

She rolled her eyes but humored me. She was good like that.

"Matt's not that good in bed."

Annie blinked. "And you thought the solution to bad in bed was to move in together?"

"Well, now I know why he's bad in bed. I'm missing a vital piece of anatomy that turns him on." I shook my head. "It was stupid. We'd been together a year, and we were at that point—"

"Gun point? Because that's the only way I'd ever move in with a guy."

"Doesn't the endless bout of one-night stands get old?" I demanded. I was secretly jealous. Or, not so secretly jealous. Annie didn't do relationships and she didn't care; and neither did the guys she regularly slept with.

"You should try it," Annie said. "And now you can."

"Ah, the bright side. Never date a guy who waxes his chest."

"Noted. So, you're feeling okay about Matt. Is that the tequila or are you just really fast at processing stuff?"

"Tequila. It numbs everything—even feelings. Truth be told, I think I'm more depressed about the job. I got to wear jeans and Converse to work."

"I know."

"And even though it wasn't very creative, I was still writing."

"I know."

9

"Stop saying *I know!*"

Annie looked completely unfazed by my outburst. "When life hands you lemons…"

"Rub them all over my open wounds and laugh?"

"Whoa with the drama."

"Stick it in a memo and fax it," I groused.

"What's a fax?"

"Really?"

"Oh, that was a boring office job reference, right?"

After our falafels, we stepped out onto 1st Avenue and she linked her arm with mine. "You don't have to have anything figured out tonight."

"Good, because I plan on drinking a lot of tequila and you know I can't think when I drink tequila."

"Let's just get plastered and pretend we're still in college. We can muddle through your crappy life tomorrow —with colossal hangovers."

"My life isn't that crappy," I protested weakly.

She sighed. "Yes. It is."

Chapter 2

Grappa [grah-pa]
1. Distilled, fermented grape skins, seeds, and stalks left over from the winemaking process.
2. Italian moonshine. It's like drinking rocket fuel.

I didn't remember the name of the bar we were in, but we were somewhere on 2nd Avenue, still on the Upper East Side. I knew this because the bartenders recognized Annie; we got drinks fast and the pool table even faster. Even though I was already swaying, I pounded tequila like it was coconut water.

"New life plan: professional tequila drinker," I said, trying to form words with a heavy tongue.

"That's not a thing. Another game of pool?" Annie asked.

"Sure. I'm so gonna beat you this time," I stated.

"Doubtful. Despite what you think, tequila does not give you super powers."

"Oh, yes it does," I said, dropping the plastic triangle on the floor. Annie laughed as she scooped up the triangle and racked the balls.

Ha. Balls.

"Am I more or less coherent than you?" I demanded.

"Less."

"How is that possible? You've been matching me drink for drink."

"I've been drinking Bud Light."

"Oooooh. Maybe I should slow down?"

"That might be a good idea."

"I'll go get a water." I sifted through the crowd towards the bar and a few minutes later I was back at the pool table.

Annie broke and sank a color ball in the corner pocket, and then leaned over to take another shot.

"Ugh, I'm gonna have to update my LinkedIn profile."

"LinkedIn is stupid and worthless."

"Not if you work in an office environment. Oh, man. What do I say?"

"You can't tell people you were fired, that's for sure."

"I didn't get fired; I was laid off. There's a difference."

"Okay."

"And I have to change my Facebook relationship status to single. I'm a failure on so many levels," I wailed.

"Facebook is almost as worthless as LinkedIn. Who says you have to update anything?"

I could hear the eye roll in her tone. "Am I as pathetic as I sound?" I demanded.

"The truth will hurt."

"Sad. How am I gonna get another job if I don't update my LinkedIn profile?"

"Your turn," Annie said.

"I need another job. Did you hear me?"

"Yeah, I heard you," she grumbled. "The whole damn bar heard you. Now take your shot."

I set my water down on the corner of the pool table. I tried to line up my pool cue, but I was having difficulty, since I was seeing the blurry outlines of things.

"Need some help?"

I looked over my shoulder at the voice.

Oh. Wow.

Six foot something guy. Dark shaggy hair. Scruff. Because of the dim bar, I couldn't tell the color of his eyes. And he wasn't wearing a polo. Flannel. He wore flannel.

My sluggish mind wondered for a moment if I'd been magically transported to Brooklyn before remembering I was on the Upper East Side playing pool. Or trying to.

"No." I rebuffed his offer, trying to focus on the shot. I scratched.

The guy laughed. "I think you need a lesson in pool."

I straightened and glared at him. "Actually, I need another drink." I took a step towards the bar.

"What are you drinking?" the guy asked.

"Tequila pineapple," Annie piped up from beside me.

I shot her a glare, but the guy smiled and headed toward the bar. "What are you doing?" I hissed at her.

She shrugged. "Time to get back on the horse. And the horse is hot. And he just went to buy you a drink. And he's wearing a flannel saddle! Totally your type!"

"He's not a horse."

13

"You're right—he's a *stallion*."

I scowled at my best friend.

"Rebound guy," she went on. "He could be your rebound guy."

"I want nothing to do with guys. I'm not ready for that."

"Why not? Matt moved on while you guys were still together—with a dude. Tit for tat, I say."

"Two guys don't make a right."

"Two guys makes a gay couple," she fired back.

I continued to glower at her even as the horse—er—hot guy came back from the bar, holding a draft beer and my tequila pineapple.

"Thanks," I said, taking it.

"No problem. You can make it up to me by losing to me in a game of pool."

I tried to sputter a witty reply, but after the day I'd had, along with what felt like an entire bottle of tequila, my neurons were no longer firing.

Annie to my rescue.

"Sibby would love that." She handed the guy her pool cue, took her drink, and moved away to sit on a bar stool, throwing herself into conversation with a guy wearing a Red Sox hat.

With no real choice, I said to the horse, "You can break."

"I'm Aidan," Hot Guy said.

"Of course you are," I muttered.

Hot name for a hot guy.

"Sibby."

"Nice to meet you, Sibby." He grinned and took a swig of his beer, then set it down so he could rack. He lined up his shot to break and maybe it was the tequila, or maybe it was because he was really hot, but I found myself getting a

14

bit warm.

He looked over at me and grinned. Without taking his eyes off me, he broke.

Jeez. Really? *Really?*

Two balls found their way into pockets. "You're solids," he called.

"Okay." I stepped toward the pool table, moving around it to try and find a decent shot. There wasn't one. I leaned over, angling my pool cue.

"You're doing it wrong," Aidan said with an insufferable grin.

"I am not," I clipped. In frustration, I let my pool cue rip and missed the ball completely.

"Told ya."

"What, are you a pool shark or something?"

"Yes." He walked close to me and whispered, "Excuse me."

"Huh?" I said stupidly. My brain went to a dopey place when Aidan's hand gently settled on my waist and moved me out of his way so he could bend over and take his shot.

I was still in a fog as he sank two more balls.

He grinned at me. "Offer still stands."

"What offer would that be?"

"Pool tips."

"Can you just beat me at this quickly so I can get back to my night with my friend?" I looked over in the direction of Annie who was no longer speaking to the guy in a Red Sox hat—she was making out with him.

"Great," I muttered.

"Are you always this cheerful?" Aidan asked with a lopsided grin. It would've been adorable if I hadn't had such a shitty day. Who was I kidding? That smile was cute with a capital OHMYGOD.

And I wanted to steer clear of it.

"I had a rough day, okay? So, I'm sorry if I'm not Miss Congeniality tonight."

He continued to grin.

"Are your friends mad that you ditched them to hang out with an angry hipster girl?"

Aidan laughed—I'd thought his grin was adorable, but it had nothing on his laugh.

Damn it.

"My friend is the guy in the Red Sox hat making out with your friend."

"Then he's definitely not upset that you ditched him," I said.

"It wouldn't appear that way, no." He cocked his head to one side as he rested his pool cue against the table. He went to one of the stools in the corner and took a seat. "Why are you having a bad day?"

I wasn't going to shout across the table to him about my pathetic existence, so I had no choice but to move to the vacant stool next to him. I was never going to see Aidan again, so I figured what the hell, might as well spill my guts.

"I got fired this morning—on a Monday—and when I went home, I walked in on my boyfriend cheating on me!" I took a long sip of my drink, and then followed it up with another couple of swallows. Buzzy tequila head felt like such a safe place.

"Hence the tequila." He set his beer down on the ledge behind us and stood up.

"Where are you going?"

"Tequila shots. Pool can't help with that kind of day, but more tequila can."

Like I needed more tequila.

Before I could say anything, Aidan left and a few minutes later came back with a tray of at least ten shots.

"All for me?" I asked sarcastically.

He laughed. "Caleb!"

The guy in the Red Sox hat managed to pull himself away from Annie's mouth just long enough to look at his friend. "What? I'm busy."

"Shots," Aidan said. "Sibby's had a bad day. You in?"

"Yeah!"

"What about you?" Aidan asked Annie. Caleb and Annie slid off their stools and joined us. We all lifted shots and downed them.

"I can't feel my face," I slurred as I pressed my fingertips to my cheeks.

"Really?" Aidan breathed.

"How many shots did we do? I've lost my ability to do math."

"Four. Each."

I looked over at Annie and Caleb, now a tangle of arms, legs, and mouths, like a weird sea creature with many tentacles. "They're not coming up for air any time soon," I said. "And I'm supposed to sleep on her futon. I can't go home. Matt is home. Matt and that guy. They were doing it on my brand new fucking sheets!"

"Wait, what? He was with a *dude?*" Aidan asked in surprise.

"Yeah. Did I forget to mention that part?"

SAMANTHA GARMAN

"Uh, yeah."

"Shouldn't matter," I stated. "Cheating is cheating, but catching him with a guy adds a whole new layer of complexity to my emotional issues."

"I get it." Aidan looked back at our friends and shook his head. "You can stay with me. I live just a couple of blocks from here."

"I don't even know you."

"We've done shots. I think that makes us friends or something."

"Or something. I'm not having sex with you just because you bought us shots. Which was—thanks."

He grinned. "Did I ask you to have sex with me?"

"Dude—I still can't feel my face and I have no idea where this conversation is going."

"Caleb is my roommate. I really don't want to hear him going at it with your friend. Solution: you come home with me—he goes home with her."

"That makes a strange sort of sense right now."

"Tequila does that. I'll take the couch and you can have my bed. No funny business, I promise."

I looked at Annie and the last thing I wanted to do was interrupt the face-sucking. "Okay, let's go."

Aidan took my hand and led me outside. "I'll send Caleb a text. He'll show it to Annie and then she won't worry that you went off into the night with a stranger."

"You're a pretty nice stranger," I commented. He didn't let go of my hand, but I found I didn't mind.

Tequila was swell.

"Sometimes, you just need someone to be really nice to you," Aidan said.

"Amen."

"So this job you had, what was it?"

"I edited textbook copy."

18

"That sounds—"

"Boring," I finished for him.

He smiled. His adorable, cute smile. "Boring, yeah. Was it your dream job or did you stumble into it?"

I shrugged. "Tripped into it, I guess. When I moved up here after college, I worked at a temp agency. One day I was sent to Hanlan and Sons and three months later, they hired me on full time."

"And the boyfriend—was he your dream boyfriend or did you trip into that, too?"

"I don't want to talk about him."

"Okay."

We walked a few blocks in silence until we arrived at an old brownstone. He unlocked the front door and let me into the vestibule before opening the second door. I followed him across the black and white tiled lobby floor to the back stairs, which he took two at a time, his long legs moving faster than mine. By the time we got to the sixth— and final—floor I was winded. Maybe I should start jogging. Or do Crossfit. Yeah, right. I'd rather do cross *sit.*

"Sorry, things are a bit messy," Aidan said, pushing open the front door.

"It's not so bad," I murmured as I looked around. Old brown couch, white walls, rock and roll posters. Cluttered, but clean—way cleaner than I expected from two guys.

"Want something to eat? Or drink?" He kicked off his shoes and threw his keys on the coffee table.

"Water would be good," I said, starting to regain feeling in my face.

Aidan headed to the kitchen, and a moment later I heard the faucet running. He returned and handed me a full glass. I took a few swallows and then clutched it in my hands.

"This is the part where I show you my room," he said.

"Oh. Yeah, sure."

His room was big enough for a double bed and not much else. There were a few pieces of clothing on the floor, but Aidan didn't make a move to pick them up. The walls were lined with classic movie posters: *Casablanca, The Godfather, Scarface*.

"Bathroom's down the hall," he said, going to his dresser drawer and pulling out a white Hanes undershirt and some boxers for me to change into.

"Thanks."

I went to the bathroom, put on Aidan's clothes, and then quickly finger brushed my teeth with some of his toothpaste to remove the taste of tequila pineapples. Turning off the bathroom light, I went into the living room and saw that Aidan was making up the couch. He'd stripped down to his boxers, showing a defined, lean build.

He was being a gentleman, but I so didn't want to be a lady.

"You should sleep in your own bed," I said.

He looked up from unfolding a blanket. "I don't mind crashing on the couch."

"That's sweet, but really, I don't feel right about kicking you out of your own bed."

"Well, there is another option."

"Yeah?"

"We could share my bed. If you promise to keep your hands to yourself."

"Me?" I choked out. We laughed and some of the awkwardness dissipated. I sighed. "I guess that would be okay—sharing your bed."

We headed back to his room and got comfortable on our designated sides, careful not to touch each other. I settled onto my back and stared at the ceiling. "Aidan?" I whispered.

"Hmm?" he asked sleepily.

"Thanks for making this shitty day not so shitty."

"You're welcome," he muttered before falling asleep.

Chapter 3

Prosecco [pro-sek-oh]

1. A sparkling white wine from the Veneto region of
northeast Italy.

2. Italy's version of champagne. Not a fan.

The moment I woke up, I knew two things. One,
Aidan was wrapped around me like a candy wrapper. And
two, even my teeth were hungover.

I'd never done the wake-up-with-a-stranger in the
morning and all that awkwardness. At twenty-seven, I
didn't really want to learn what it was like. I gently
removed Aidan's arm from across my stomach. Thankfully,

he didn't stir. He looked good when he slept. Really good. I had to stifle the urge to lean over and stick my finger in one of his cheek dimples.

Yeah. The dude had *dimples*.

Before that feeling overtook me, I got up, changed back into my clothes, and tiptoed out into the living room. Everything was quiet and I wondered if that meant Caleb hadn't returned yet. Knowing Annie, she'd kick him out as soon as she woke up. At least she let her conquests stay the night. Nice of her.

Riffling through my wallet, I found $38.43 and left it on the coffee table. I scribbled on a piece of junk mail, *Thanks for the tequila* before slipping out of his apartment.

I had a bajillion missed messages and voicemails. All from Matt. I continued to ignore them. I'd turned off my phone the previous night. Unfortunately, my silence hadn't been a deterrent to him.

I texted Annie.

Me: Diner? Now?

A few seconds later, my phone vibrated.

Annie: Corner of 86th and 1st. 10 minutes.

I was close to the diner, and when I arrived there was a lull in customers, so I managed to score an empty booth right away. I ordered two cups of shitty, watered-down diner coffee, sipping mine while waiting for Annie. She strolled in a few minutes later, wearing large Old-Holly-wood style sunglasses. She slid into her seat and said, "You look like I feel."

"That good, huh? At least I didn't throw up."

"I'm surprised. You were blitzed." She took off her sunglasses and set them aside, exposing bloodshot eyes and reaching for her cup of coffee. "So what happened with you and Aidan?"

"Nothing. What happened with you and Caleb?"

She grinned. "A lady doesn't kiss and tell."

"You're not a lady."

"Damn right. We hooked up."

"Did you exchange phone numbers?"

"Nope. Did you exchange numbers with Aidan?"

I shook my head. The waitress came over, snapping her gum. We ordered without even looking at the menu. Diner food was standard in New York City. After my third cup of coffee, I was beginning to feel a little less zombified. I started thinking about my game plan for the day.

"I have to go back to Brooklyn and deal with the apartment and Matt. But I don't want to deal with Matt."

"It's a Tuesday—he'll be at work."

"That's the hope. Wouldn't it be nice if I could wave a magic wand and all of that cheating bastard's stuff would be out of my place?"

"That would be nice, but what are you actually gonna do about him?"

The waitress set down a stack of pancakes in front of me and eggs in front of Annie. I picked up my fork and said, "I really have no idea."

I walked into my apartment and listened for any unusual sounds. There were no laughs coming from the bedroom, which made me thank my unlucky stars.

Matt's clothes were still in the drawers, his shoes still by the door. My first order of business was to call a locksmith. The apartment was a perfect one bedroom. It was rent controlled, and had been mine before Matt moved in. He cheated, so he would be the one to move out.

While Matt was at work and I waited for the locksmith, I loaded up all of his stuff and shoved it haphazardly into suitcases, plastic bags, and boxes. I stripped the bed of sheets now stained with betrayal…and something else.

YUCK.

Matt could have them.

By four in the afternoon the apartment was fairly cleaned out, all of Matt's belongings were in the hallway, the locksmith was gone, and I was nursing a glass of wine. Now that I was unemployed and boyfriend-less, there was no one to care if I became a lush. Becoming a lush was rapidly turning into my new life goal.

I heard a stream of curses as Matt saw his belongings in the hallway, followed by an attempt to use his old key in the new lock.

"Sibby? Are you home?" Matt called, pounding on the door.

"Go away!" I shouted. "You don't live here anymore!"

"Come on Sib, open the door!"

"No! Take your crap and go! I gave you and your new boy a present. Enjoy the sheets, you tool!"

I continued to drink and turned on the TV, cranking the volume as the knocking on the door intensified. Eventually, Matt got bored and gave up, and I got drunk enough to pass out.

I woke up around 11:00 p.m. My mouth was a bit dry, but I seemed to have slept off any oncoming hangover. I got myself a glass of water and went to the front door. Without removing the chain, I opened the door and peered out into the hallway. No sign of Matt or his stuff. I gave a sigh of relief. I wouldn't have to deal with him if I didn't have to see him.

There was no food in the fridge, so I put on my skull-and-crossbones leggings and grabbed my purse. I headed to the corner bodega and nabbed some staples.

By which I mean junk food. Lots and lots of junk food.

Epic sugar coma, here I come.

I shoved the Matt situation back into a closet in my mind and closed the door. I'd deal with the butt-load of issues from his betrayal later. I hadn't given much thought about the job I'd lost. It was a paycheck, but not much else. I'd been a theater major in college with a creative writing minor, but when I moved to New York I needed a job that paid. Editing psychology textbook copy wasn't very fulfilling, but it was steady income. End of story.

I got back to the apartment and made myself some dinner. My phone buzzed and I grimaced, thinking it was Matt. I had deleted all his messages and voicemails. There was no point listening to them. What could he say? Sorry I cheated? Sorry you caught me? Sorry you don't have a penis?

Man, I needed new shoes to go with all my baggage.

It wasn't Matt, it was Annie.

"Hey."

"Where are you?" she demanded.

"My apartment."

"Come out."

"What? Are you crazy? It's almost midnight."

"Come on. You're single now."

"I'm tired."

"You're not."

"I am," I insisted. "I started drinking early and already passed out once. I made some food and then I plan on going back to bed."

"Wow, that's what I call depression."

"I'm not gonna even deny it."

"You hear from Matt?" she asked.

"He came by earlier, but I had already thrown his stuff out into the hall and had the locks changed. He's gone now."

"Way to be proactive. You sound remarkably composed. Shouldn't you cry over your broken heart or something?"

I paused. "You'd think so, huh? I still don't really know what to think—or feel, for that matter."

"Hmmm."

"That was a loaded *hmmm*."

"I wonder if your heart is even broken at all, or if it's just your ego."

"Broken ego?" I mulled. "Yeah, sounds about right. How did I not know he was gay? Come to think of it— how did *you* not know he was gay?"

"It wasn't like he did anything flamboyant. And the guy is into sports."

"I feel like an idiot," I said. "Yeah, this is all about my pride."

She was quiet for a second. "If you change your mind and want to come out—"

"Thanks, but I think I'm in for the night. I've got an early morning appointment tomorrow."

"Oh? For what?"

"I'm going to see the gynecologist—and let me tell you, I'm so not looking forward to *that* conversation."

"Just do it before you're in the stirrups," she recommended. "It's hard to keep your dignity when your legs are spread."

"You would know," I teased.

"Bitch. I'll allow it, though. Your life kinda sucks."

"Great. Now you pity me."

"Do something nice for yourself after the appointment. Get a mani-pedi, or a massage."

"I'm getting my hair cut."

"Tell them your story and maybe you'll get a free scalp massage. Just do me a favor. Don't chop off all your hair. No pixie cuts."

"I did that once and looked like a Q-tip head. No danger of that happening again."

"What about that new hipster haircut—where half your head is shaved and half of it is long?"

"No. I'm just getting a regular haircut."

"Promise me."

"I promise."

"Okay. How about I come to Brooklyn in the next few days and hang out. We can watch bad movies and eat junk food."

"You'd come to Brooklyn? For me?"

"What can I say? I'm a really good friend."

I laughed. "Yeah. You are."

"You should paint," Annie said.

I looked around the living room. The walls were stark white, like I'd never really moved in. No posters or framed photos. "Yeah, I should paint." I peeled the label off my beer bottle. "It was weird, sleeping alone.

I had to sleep in the middle of the bed at a diagonal."

"How did that go?"

"Around 3:00 a.m. I got up to take a sleeping pill."

"I think that's what killed Judy."

"Great, the Judy Garland jokes have started."

"Sorry, it was just too easy." Annie reached for the plate of lukewarm nachos.

"Well, thanks for not wearing kid gloves."

"One day, you'll laugh about everything."

"Promise?"

"Yeah. Trust me."

"Okay." I let out a deep sigh and then changed the conversation. "Tell me about your night out."

Annie scowled. "I didn't score."

"No?"

"I spent most of my night talking to this really cute guy, and I was totally prepared to take him home. Then he tells me that he's a vegetarian. Soyfucker." She frowned in disgust. "I have standards, ya know?"

"You've got a weird check list."

"I'm a chef and bacon is my favorite food group. I'm forgiving of a lot of flaws, but not that one."

"Fair enough."

"So, have you started thinking about a new job yet?"

"Not yet," I evaded.

"You need money, right?"

"Who doesn't need money? I have a little bit in savings to get me by for a while."

"It won't be enough if you keep drinking the way you have been."

"Whose fault is that?" I demanded. "You're a bad influence."

"I'm a *great* influence."

"Whatever."

She looked at me. "What are you gonna do?"

"I don't know. The idea of networking, calling head hunters, applying to endless jobs in the field that I've been working in for the past five years is giving me hives."

"Dramatic much?"

"Hello. Theater major."

"Yeah, I recall."

When I was studying theater in school, Annie had come to every one of my shows. There had been a lot of them—and most of them were pretty bad.

God bless her.

"I don't want to edit textbook copy—and I don't think I want to work in an office again."

"All you've ever done is work in offices. What else are you qualified to do?"

"This is a chance, Annie, a chance to do something different. What is it people say when shit goes wrong? A blessing in disguise? That's what this is."

"So, what do you wanna do with your life?"

"I have absolutely no idea."

"Well, as long as you have a plan…" she teased.

"I don't have one of those either. I'm jobless, boyfriend-less, plan-less."

"You're not freaking out, are you? That's so unlike you."

"I'm freaked out because I'm *not* freaking out."

"Still no tears for Matt?"

"Nope. It's like, none of the water in my body will come out of my eyeballs."

I went into the kitchen and grabbed two more beers. I handed her one and she said, "So, are you gonna sit around and collect unemployment while trying to figure out your life?"

"For the time being. But unemployment doesn't go very far. I won't even be able to afford Thai takeout. And besides, I think I'm one of those people that needs to be doing something. If I don't, I'll go crazy."

"You mean being a slug doesn't work for you?"

"Exactly," I said. "Can I ask you a favor?"

"What?"

"Will you sleep here tonight?"

"Okay, but I'm the big spoon."

The next morning, I sent Annie off to work with a cup of coffee in a travel mug and a full stomach. I felt like a housewife in the fifties. After I puttered around a bit on my computer, I finally got serious.

LinkedIn.

Just to see what was out there in the way of jobs. Not that I knew what kind of job I wanted. It was overwhelming and I didn't even know where to start or what to look for. My phone vibrated. Matt. The guy just wasn't getting it. But instead of ignoring him this time, I answered.

"What?"

"Sibby, can we please talk?" Matt asked, sounding desperate.

Good.

"What do you want to talk about? You wanted out of

our relationship, and instead of being a man and coming clean with me about it, you had sex with someone in our apartment—on our *brand new sheets*. That we got on sale. At Pottery Barn. You know how much I love Pottery Barn!"

"I'm sorry—"

"Yeah, well, it's too little, too late! Stop calling me."

I hung up on him and then blocked his number, grabbed my keys, and went to go find some paint.

Annie squinted and frowned, cocking her head to one side in confusion. "I know you said you wanted to paint, but this is not what I thought you'd do. It looks like you hired a kindergartener to throw paint on a wall."

I'd gotten a headache from the paint fumes, so the windows were open, and I had no interest in finishing the rest of the living room. That one painted wall would remain, to remind me of my day of infamy; to remind me that I needed some color in my colorless life. I was certainly feeling poetic.

"Were you sober when you did this?"

"Uhmmm," I hedged. I'd had tequila with a side of coffee. Patron Espresso. I was wired and tipsy.

It was phenomenal.

"You've become a tequila monster."

"There are worse things, I suppose. So, do you like it?"

"It's weird. But you're weird, so it makes sense. And yes, I like it."

I smiled and we took a seat on the couch. "I want a new bed. And new towels. New everything to replace all the stuff I bought with Matt."

"That costs money."

"Yeah, I don't think unemployment will cover that."

"Which brings me to this; you know when my boss Heather throws those luncheons and I have to hire cater waiters?"

"I don't want to cater waiter. I hate bowties."

Annie rolled her eyes. "Wasn't gonna ask you to be a cater waiter. Besides, it's way part-time. You'd make more on unemployment. No, one of Heather's cater waiters works at an Italian restaurant in the West Village, but he's leaving to tour with a Midwestern theater company. They have to hire his replacement."

"Huh," I said.

"I threw out your name and history."

"History?"

"Yeah, you waited tables."

"In college," I pointed out. "At a barbecue joint. I was always covered in barbecue sauce."

"Oh…yeah. Might have forgotten about that."

"Looked like a freakin' extra from *Braveheart*," I muttered. "Besides, I don't know crap about Italian food."

"You need money, yes?"

"Yes."

"You don't want to work in an office or go back to editing textbook copy."

"That's true."

"So, wait tables while you figure out what you really want to do."

I went quiet.

"Is this a pride thing? You don't want to be a twenty-seven-year-old waitress? Rachel on *Friends* did it."

"She has better hair than me. And that was a TV show. Her life magically worked out because writers wrote that her life worked out. And, oh, yeah, she's fictional."

"Lots of artists do the waiting tables thing while pursuing their art."

"Yeah, but I'm not pursuing art."

"What are you talking about?" She pointed to the wall. "You're a painter."

My sigh was labored. "How does one even make a resume for a restaurant?"

"I don't know. Maybe they'll just make you carry a tray of drinks. Kind of like an audition."

"Um, I spill things. I'm totally screwed."

Jessica, the general manager at Antonio's stared at me. I tried not to twitch. Her brown eyes surveyed me. I was wearing my black glasses, skinny-leg jeans and checkered shirt, and my dark, somewhat frizzy hair was pulled back into a ponytail.

"You're a Hipster," she said finally.

"No, I…Yes." I paused. "Please don't hold that against me."

She smiled faintly. "You're a friend of Tom's?"

"Friend of a friend," I corrected. "He cater waiters for my best friend."

"You've worked in a restaurant before?"

"A barbecue joint."

"You like people?"

"Sure?"

Her brown eyes flared with humor. "Do you know anything about Italian food or Italian wine?"

"I can fake anything."

Jess raised an eyebrow. I smiled.

"You're an actor."

"Writer," I amended.

"Same thing."

"Not the same thing at all."

She leaned back in her chair. "I like you."

I smiled, hoping that meant I had the job.

"Can you start training tomorrow?"

"Yes."

"Come in at four. We're only open for dinner. If you survive training, you'll work four shifts a week. Got it?"

Survive training?

"Got it."

"Jess!" a male voice called. "I can't find the new Barbaresco shipment!"

"I got it," Jess yelled back, standing up. "Come meet our newest employee!"

I heard someone tromping up the stairs and a tall, lean, familiar body appeared in the doorway of the dining room.

"Sibby, meet our assistant manager, Aidan."

Chapter 4

Tartufo [tar-too-foh]

   1. Italian for "truffle".

   2. You know it's a fungus, right?

    I waited until Jess left us alone to go tend to the lost wine shipment before I looked skyward and said, "You've got to be kidding me. What are you doing here?"

    "I work here," Aidan, hot guy from the other night, said. "What are *you* doing here?"

    "I work here now, too."

    "No more textbook editing?"

    "I'm making a change. How do you remember that,

anyway? I thought you were too drunk to remember much of anything."

"You were drunker than me. I was pretty sober actually."

I moaned. "Really? Even after the shots?"

"Kind of hurt my ego when you snuck out of my apartment before I woke up. Didn't even kiss me goodbye." His smile was slow.

I shook my head. "This is bad."

"Why?"

"How we met was—embarrassing. No one needs to know about my drunken idiocy."

"You mean, they shouldn't know that we spooned the night we met?"

"Exactly."

"This isn't like working in an office, Sibby. Co-workers can date."

I held up my hand. "First of all, we aren't co-workers, you're technically my boss. Second of all, we're not dating. And D, did you get the money I left on your coffee table? For the shots?"

"All thirty-eight dollars of it?" His grin was still in place.

"Thirty-eight dollars and *some change*," I reminded him.

"Yeah, I got it." We stared at each other for a long moment. Aidan shifted his stance. "Well, if you're working here, then I should give you the menu descriptions."

"Excuse me?" I blinked.

"Menu descriptions, so you know what's in the food." He gestured for me to follow him to the host stand. He riffled through a stack of papers before handing me a packet. I flipped through it.

"You're kidding, right? This is like thirty pages of intensive reading."

He smiled. "We like our guests to have options."

"The menu is huge."

"Yep."

"I feel like I need a PhD in food to work here."

"There are wine descriptions in there, too."

"Joy," I muttered.

"The thing about wine, though, is you have to taste it so you can make notes and speak confidently about it. Why don't you stick around and I'll take you through a tasting?"

I raised an eyebrow. "Are you suggesting that as my boss, or as the guy who got me drunk after I had the worst day of my life?"

He grinned. "Your boss."

"Damn it. Okay. Bring on the wine." We headed to the bar and he pulled out two wine glasses and some bottles. "Aidan?"

"Yeah?" He looked at me.

"What did Jessica mean when she said *survive training*?"

"The chef is a bit…high strung."

"High strung?"

"Passionate."

"Passionate?"

"Okay, he yells a lot," he explained. "And sometimes he throws dishes."

"*What?*"

"Not *at* anyone. Shit, please don't quit before you start."

I shook my head, wondering what mess I was walking into. I turned to the last page with the list of wines. "There are at least fifteen wines by the glass on here."

"Yep," Aidan agreed.

"Isn't that overkill?"

"Yep."

"I'm gonna be drunk by the time we're done."

He grinned. "Hope so."

Aidan poured me my first taste of a red. I put it to my nose and smelled it, swirling it around, pretending to know what I was doing. I was a beer and tequila kind of girl. Sometimes bourbon. I didn't know squat about wine.

"Caleb is into Annie," Aidan said suddenly.

"This is personal talk," I said as I took a sip. I wrote down ridiculous descriptions: big, bold, spicy, leathery.

People just made up wine descriptions, right?

"You never said we couldn't be personal. Besides, personal is good."

"Boundaries, Aidan. Boundaries are necessary." I glowered at him.

"There's no one here," he said. "The servers don't come in to set up for another hour. We can talk about personal stuff all you want."

"But I don't *want* to talk about personal stuff."

Aidan ignored me completely. "I'll go first."

"Please, don't." He needed to stay "the guy from the bar" or "my new manager". Those boxes made sense to me. Details about his life would make him a real person. I couldn't have that.

"You're harsh. Okay, I won't talk about myself. Annie kicked Caleb out the next morning, sans phone number."

"So, we're not gonna talk about personal stuff then?" I said with blatant sarcasm.

"Oh come on, I'm not asking about you. I'm asking about your friend for my friend."

I sighed. "Annie doesn't do repeats."

"Excuse me?"

"Repeats. She bags them once and sends them on their way. That's as personal as *she* gets."

"Caleb wasn't hoping for a repeat performance. Or he was, but only after he took her on a date."

I frowned. "Date? Really."

"Really."

"I find that hard to believe."

"Clearly."

"Annie would have a hard time believing that, too."

"Believe it or not, it's true. So if I pass along Caleb's number to you, and you give it to Annie…"

"She's not going to call him," I vowed. "And do me a favor. Please don't tell Caleb that I work here. Let's keep real life separate from work life."

He shook his head and sighed. "You gonna finish that little taste or dump it out?"

I looked affronted. "One thing I do know about wine; you never waste a sip."

A few days later, Jess introduced me to a tall, thin guy with spiky blond hair and diamond studs in his ears. "Zeb, this is our newest recruit, Sibby."

"Hi," I said, holding out my hand, which he shook.

"Zeb is going to train you tonight," Jess said.

"I am? That's news to me."

"Zeb…"

"She looks young and fresh. I might destroy that with my bitchiness."

Jess looked at me. "Don't believe anything he says." She walked away, leaving me alone with Zeb.

"Come on, I'll give you the grand tour of this place."
Zeb took me through the front dining room and began to
show me the layout of the restaurant, complete with table
numbers. "And then we have a back room," he said,
leading me past the kitchen into a courtyard area. The
floor was uneven cobblestone, and there was a large unlit
gas fireplace at the back.

"Canvas roof," Zeb explained. "So we can heat it in
the winter and cool it in summer. But on perfect days like
today…" He gestured to sunlight shining down on us.

"Nice," I said.

An hour later, I heard yelling in French, followed by the
sound of breaking dishes. I glanced at Zeb. He seemed
remarkably unruffled. Like it was an ordinary occurrence. I
could feel the stress streaming from the kitchen.

"This is an Italian restaurant, right?" I asked him.

"Yes."

"Then why is the chef French?"

"Sibby, let me give you a piece of advice," Zeb said.
"This is Antonio's. If it makes sense, it doesn't happen
here. Antonio's is the anti-logic. Trust me, this is a drop in
the bucket."

"Yikes."

"Each restaurant has its own brand of crazy. I don't
even notice it anymore, to be honest."

"Wow."

"The shifts are short and the money is good. And no
lunch or brunch. We put up with a lot for those sorts of
perks."

"What other things do I have to look forward to?" I
demanded.

He thought for a minute. "No, I'm not going to tell
you."

"Why not?"

He grinned. "More fun that way."

"For you, maybe."

"Definitely for me."

"Are you hiding horns under that blond hair?"

Zeb laughed. "So, what's your story?"

"Story?"

"Yeah, like, I'm in college, so I work a few shifts around my class schedule. What about you?"

"You're still in college?"

"I keep changing my major," Zeb explained. "It's why I'm a twenty-eight-year-old junior. Are you an actor who has to go on a bunch of auditions? Something like that?"

"Oh, that kind of story," I said slowly and then figured, *what the hell?* "I got laid off from my office gig editing text-book copy."

"And instead of getting another job editing textbook copy you decided to work in a restaurant?"

"I'm hoping for a new direction," I said. "You ever work in an office?"

"God, no. The idea of working in an office makes me want to put a bullet in my brain. Or drink an entire bottle of soda and down some Pop Rocks." He looked at me. "I have one mode. It's called *sarcasm*."

I raised an eyebrow. "Change kinda happened to me. I figured I might as well embrace it. What do I have to lose?"

"Uhm. Your sanity."

"I've worked in a restaurant before. Long ago, in a galaxy far, far away…"

"Have you ever worked at a restaurant in New York City?" He stared at me and I shook my head. "Then pay attention, because you'll want to remember what I'm about to say: People are insane. Like, crazy cat-lady insane. You're going to have to guide them through this journey we call dinner. They want the impossible. They want things without knowing what they want. They're going to ask stupid questions, like, whether there is gluten in pasta, and you're going to have to smile and try not to punch them in the face. You're going to have to bring them what they asked for, and listen when they tell you that they didn't order what they ordered. You're going to want to drink. A lot. But we've got a good group here, and both Aidan and Jess are awesome managers."

At the mention of Aidan's name, my stomach felt like it dropped out of my body and landed on the floor.

"Especially Aidan. He's a good guy. And he's fucking hot. I'm gay, by the way."

"Yeah, I kinda already got that."

"You met Aidan, right?"

I nodded, struggling to get air into my lungs. "He went through a wine tasting with me the other day."

"Excellent. That's one less thing I have to do."

"You don't like training people, do you?" I asked.

"Hate it, actually. I try and scare the newbs off, but Jess keeps giving me people to train. Makes no sense."

"Maybe you're the first test. If people get by you that means they have real staying power."

"Have I scared you off?"

"Not yet."

"Damn. I need to up my game."

43

I hadn't spoken to Annie since I'd been hired a week ago. She had left town with her boss to go to the Hamptons and cook a dinner party. She'd only just gotten back into the city that morning. We met in neutral territory, a bar around the Union Square area, half the distance between the Upper East Side and Brooklyn. Location mattered to New Yorkers.

"Cheers," Annie said, clinking her martini against mine. "You made it through training."

"I did."

I wasn't sure how I'd done it. Maybe it was because I'd taken Zeb's advice and ignored the chef. I had also ignored Aidan, though he was almost un-ignorable. He was super dreamy.

I was making myself sick to my stomach.

Annie set her drink down and said, "Tell me about stuff."

I held up my right pointer finger. It was covered in a roll of Band-Aids. She frowned. "What happened?"

"Foil finger. From practicing opening wine bottles and nicking myself."

"You're like, really cool, you know that?" Annie said sarcastically.

"I never had to open wine bottles at the barbecue joint. It was just beer and sweet tea."

"Point taken."

I grinned and paused for dramatic effect. "Aidan is my manager."

Annie's blue eyes widened comically. "*Aidan* Aidan? Caleb's friend? The guy you slept with but didn't sleep with?"

"That would be the one," I affirmed.

"That's New York for you."

"Right?"

"And you didn't think to call me immediately?" Annie asked.

"I wanted to see your face."

"You're a bitch."

"That I am," I agreed.

"So, have you kissed him yet?"

"What!" I shouted. "Are you insane? I can't do that."

"Why not? You know you want to."

"Do not."

"Do too."

"Do not!"

She rolled her eyes and then her face shifted into a look of panic. "Wait, did Aidan tell Caleb that you two work together?"

"Worried about Caleb finding you, huh?'"

"No!" She paused. "Maybe."

"I told Aidan he's not allowed to tell Caleb."

"What is this, junior high?"

"You tell me. According to Aidan, Caleb wants to ask you out on a date."

"I don't get it. I already gave up the goods."

"Yes, I pointed that out. You know, it's possible he actually likes you."

"Huh. But I don't go on dates."

"What about when we were in college?"

"Dinner at Moe's doesn't count."

We both fell silent. Annie stared into her martini and I took a sip of mine, and by tacit agreement, we decided not to talk about Aidan or Caleb anymore.

"Heard from Matt?"

I shook my head. "Not since I blocked his number."

"No emails?"

I shrugged. "I haven't checked my spam folder, so I have no idea."

"Do you have feelings, like at all?" Annie wondered in dismay. "I mean, you haven't wallowed or cried, or left your house with chocolate on your face or anything. You lost a job and a boyfriend in one day. What are you, a cyborg?"

"Maybe I'm a really good compartmentalizer. Ever think of that?" She raised an eyebrow and stared me down. "I don't know, Annie," I said quietly. "I think about the office job I no longer go to and I wonder how I managed to last as long as I did. The restaurant is taking some getting used to, but I don't have to ride the subway at rush hour. Do you know how amazing that is?"

"And what about Matt?"

"No use crying over an ex's hidden sexuality."

She blinked. "You're being way too mature about this. Cry! Scream! Get a tattoo or something! Go off the rails!"

"Tattoo? I'm thinkin'…no."

"Let's pierce your nose!" She reached for the olive laden toothpick in her martini glass.

I covered my nose in a protective gesture. "Back away from the nose. It's my one feature I'm immensely proud of. Why are you so unruly?"

"Sorry. This is my second martini."

"Second?"

"I got a head start while I waited for you."

"Shit, I better catch up."

I weeble-wobbled home around 2:00 a.m. It was a weeknight. My life, once a boring routine of nine to five was now, at the very least, not that. If I wanted to stay out on a school night, I could. If I wanted to go to the post office during the day, I didn't have to go on my lunch break. It was weird. Daylight hours were mine.

I climbed the stairs of my apartment building, and all my good feelings disappeared.

Matt was on his butt, leaning against the wall. Asleep.

I wanted to punt him. I settled for nudging him with my foot. When he didn't stir, I gave in to my impulse and kicked him.

Hard.

He moaned, his eyes flying open. "Sibby," he said, jumping to his feet.

"Go away," I said, sticking my key in the lock.

"I want to talk."

"You're like an alley cat that won't go away. I had the locks changed; I blocked your phone number. Don't you get it?" I asked. "I don't want to talk."

"I screwed up!"

"Understatement! Mayday, mayday! Eject, eject!" I finally got the door open and shoved my way into the apartment. Matt tried to follow, but I elbowed him back. "Go. Away. Or I'm calling the cops!"

"You won't call the cops."

I glared at him. "Try me."

"Sibby, I really want to talk."

"Why?" I stated. "I don't need to hear what you have to say. Nothing you say is going to change the fact that I caught you cheating on me with some random dude!"

"He's not random. His name is Taylor."

Annoyance morphed into drunken rage. "You're a *putz*, you know that?"

"I—"

"And a *schmuck*! You're a *schmutz!* Oh, wait. That's actually a Yiddish word and doesn't mean what I want it to mean."

"Are you drunk?"

"None of your damn business! Stop loitering in my hallway."

I slammed the door in his face.

Chapter 5

Al dente [ahl-den-teh]:

1. Literally, to the tooth; a term for slightly under-cooked pasta.

2. Your pasta is not crunchy. No need to send it back to the kitchen and have them remake it. Seriously.

"Okay, explain to me the different meats on the meat platter—and what animal they come from," Annie said, my menu description packet on her lap. She took a sip of beer while she waited for me to answer.

"Uhm…hold on, give me a moment," I said, pacing across my living room floor.

"Damn. There is so much information in here. How are you supposed to memorize all this?" she demanded.

"Shhh."

"But—"

"No more pep talks from you."

"A nice Jewish girl works in an Italian restaurant…It's like the beginning of a really good joke."

"Can we just go over the food descriptions, please?"

"Yes," she agreed. "Meat platter…"

"Pork, pork, and more pork."

"Rah, rah, rah!" she cheered.

"I'm never going to remember this entire menu. *Antipasti, insalatas, pastas, secondi, contorni, dolci.* That's like— thousands of ingredients."

Annie laughed. "What are your basic ingredients of Italian cooking?"

"Pork. But we established that already. Garlic…and cheese."

"Three staples to Italian cooking. There ya go."

"Homemade pastas, homemade desserts, aperitifs, digestifs. The frickin' barbecue restaurant had about fifteen items on the entire menu. And no one had food allergies; no one was worried about gluten or sugar. Now, it's apparently cool to be allergic to everything except kale and water."

"Uh, it's not cool. Not cool at all. Stop procrastinating. Meat platter: go!"

"I remember them! Soppressata, speck, coppa, prosciutto, bresaola. All from the pig. Except for the bresaola. That's from a cow."

"Very good. Next question: are you still avoiding Aidan?"

"That's not a food question."

"No, but it's much more interesting."

"I wish he wasn't so pretty."

"Catch yourself staring at him?"

"All the time. He walks by and it's like—instant brain static."

"If I was a terrible best friend, I'd place bets to see how long you're able to keep your pants on around him."

"I would never take a bet like that," I scoffed.

"Because you know you'd lose."

I sighed. "Probably."

My first shift. Flying solo. My very own section. My apron was new and starched, my black button-down relatively wrinkle free, and my wily, frizzy hair pulled back in the semblance of a ponytail.

Five minutes after we opened, the hostess walked over with one customer. She tried to seat the tall, gaunt woman at a table for two at the banquette, but the woman wasn't having any of it.

"That one. I want that table," she said, pointing at a table for four.

"Are you expecting anyone to join you?" the sweet, young hostess asked.

The woman glared at her. "No."

"Oh. Well, we really need that table for four."

"The restaurant is empty. Why can't I just sit there?" the woman demanded.

The harassed hostess mumbled something under her breath, blushed and let the woman have her way. I waited for a minute, wanting the woman to get comfortable, but before I could approach her, she held up her hand and snapped at me.

Snapped. At. Me.

"Excuse me? I don't have all day."

I hastened to her and said, "May I bring you some water?"

"You may," she said loftily. "No ice, three slices of lemon, and a straw. Also I'd like some bread, butter, salt, pepper, and Parmesan. I'll order when you return." Her face was screwed up in a picture of annoyance.

It was my first table in my own section ever and already my patience was being tested.

"Sure thing," I said. I left to do The Queen's bidding, and asked a busser to bring her all the ingredients she had ordered to apparently make her own appetizer.

I dropped off the water along with the accompaniments and said, "The bread will be right out. He's just cutting it. Do you need more time with the menu? Have any questions?"

Her nostrils flared, as if she was angry that she had to wait for anything. What was with her?

"The risotto balls, are they vegetarian?"

I smiled. "Yes, they are."

"I'll have those. And the roast kale salad, but I want it raw, not cooked, and add cheese but hold the dressing."

I was thrown into the deep end—on my very first day. Some kind of karmic bullshit, right?

"Got it," I said, taking her menu. "Would you like something to drink?"

"Just a decaf cappuccino. Make sure it's decaf."

"Absolutely." I went to the computer by the coffee

station where Zeb was folding napkins. "Can I ask you if I'm putting this order in right? It's a bit complicated."

Zeb stopped folding his napkins and came to my side. "Jesus. Why can't people like that stay home?"

"Seriously. Anyway, she's vegetarian, so she ordered the risotto balls."

Zeb grinned. "And you let her? With a straight face?"

"What? Wait...oh my God. They're not vegetarian?"

"A little chicken stock won't kill her."

"So I shouldn't tell her?"

"Oh, no, honey, she won't know the difference."

"Okay, well I have to make her a decaf cappuccino. She stressed that it *must* be decaf."

Zeb's eyes twinkled with server power. "She's *so* not getting decaf."

"What if it stops her heart?" I asked.

"We'll be doing the world a favor. Hopefully she hasn't procreated." He looked at me. "It's possible it's time for me to leave the hospitality industry."

The busser came back from dropping off bread and said to me, "She's asking for her decaf cappuccino."

I grinned. It was pure evil. "She'll get it."

And on my very first night, I had become a server of justice.

"So, like, what's the difference between calamari and

octopus?" the girl asked. She twirled a strand of bleached blond hair around a finger and smacked pink bubble gum while she gazed at me with questioning brown eyes.

"The difference between calamari and octopus?" I repeated. "Really?"

She nodded. "Like, is it just that they're cooked differently, or what?"

"They're two different animals."

"They are?"

"Calamari is squid. And octopus is…octopus."

"Oh." She paused. "I don't get it."

Six hours later, my first shift was over. I had somehow managed to avoid going into the kitchen, thus avoiding the temperamental French chef.

"First night done. How do you feel?" Aidan asked.

I pretended to check my body for wounds. "Okay, I think. I'm not bleeding out. Most people were really nice."

"Yeah?"

"Yeah. Except for my first table. *Horrible* human being. And she tipped 16.35%. If you're a terrible person, you should have to tip more. To ensure good karma."

"Good luck enforcing that," he said.

"And then there was the girl who didn't know the difference between calamari and octopus."

"You keep a straight face?"

"Barely."

He laughed. "Up for a celebratory drink?"

I raised an eyebrow. "With you?"

"Who else?" he demanded.

"Blurring those lines, are ya?"

"If you'll let me," he said. Two customers were on their way out and Aidan momentarily turned his attention away from me to wish them goodnight. While he was distracted,

I skipped downstairs to change clothes. It was important to keep my distance.

"Good job tonight," Natalie said, slinging her large purse over her shoulder. She was gorgeous and lithe—she had the body of a dancer. Her black hair was twirled up into a fancy bun and her half-Asian heritage was striking. She also still looked amazing and fresh.

I was greasy and hungry.

"Thanks," I said.

"What train do you take?" she asked.

"The L."

"I take the F. Wanna walk to 6th with me? Grab a slice of pizza?"

I smiled. "Sure, sounds good."

We headed up the stairs to the main floor and Natalie waved to Aidan. "Bye, Aidan. See ya later."

"Bye," he said, his eyes darting to me.

Did I detect disappointment on his face?

"God, he's so hot," Natalie muttered when we were outside, headed for greasy, cheesy perfection.

"You think so?" I asked, feigning nonchalance.

She looked at me like I was an alien from Planet Blind. "Jesus, that guy…he's so sexy. And nice."

"Such a rare combo."

"Seriously. I'm contemplating making a move. I know he's our manager, but he goes out drinking with us all the time. Maybe I should make a drunk move?" She looked at me. "You're judging me now, aren't you?"

I forced out a laugh. "No, not at all." Suddenly, I wasn't hungry for pizza—a knot of jealousy had invaded my stomach.

"Hey, you know what, I totally forgot I need to get home," I said. "Can we grab pizza another time?"

Natalie nodded. "Sure. See ya later!"

"You ready?" Zeb asked.

"No," I said. "I can't do this."

He rested his hands on my shoulders. "You can, and you will."

"I don't know the menu well enough."

"Not true. You passed your food test. You even got the extra credit question right."

"I'll fuck up."

"Probably," he agreed. "But you did fine this week."

"Saturday nights are not the same as Mondays and Tuesdays," I argued. "Even I know that."

"Pull it together, woman! It's just food. You're not curing cancer. People don't die from us doing our jobs… not if they have EpiPens anyway."

I took a deep breath.

"Good. Now slap a smile on your face!"

My lips pulled into a grimace and Zeb shook his head. "Not like that—that will scare people. You'll be okay. I'm right next to you if you get too deep in the weeds."

The rush lasted three hours. Customers just kept coming. By 11:00 p.m. I was exhausted, my feet hurt, and I could barely find the energy to speak. I was in desperate need of a drink.

"You okay?" Jess asked me as I handed her my stack of table receipts for the evening.

I managed to nod.

"Poor thing. You've been rendered speechless."

I nodded again, more vigorously this time.

"The bar next door is one of our local haunts. They always hook us up."

"Who always hooks us up?" Zeb asked, setting his checkout down in front of Jess.

"The bartenders at Johnny's."

"Ah, yes, double pours, but they only charge us for singles. Awesome burgers, too."

"Why didn't you tell me this at the beginning of my night? So I could have something to look forward to?" I asked, my tongue finally able to form words. My head was buzzing from all the stimuli.

He grinned. "You had to make it through your first Saturday before we could indoctrinate you."

"I'm getting a burger with the works."

"Bacon?" Zeb asked.

"Duh. I'm so not kosher."

"You coming after you close?" Zeb asked Jess.

"Nope. I got a bottle of wine and a hot man waiting at home for me."

"You're so domestic it's gross," Zeb said.

"I know," Jess said with a wide grin.

I changed clothes quickly and grabbed my stuff, waiting for Zeb at the front of the restaurant. We walked next door, finding a long wood table and quickly placing our drink and food orders.

"You okay?" Zeb asked.

"Yeah, but Katrina still won't talk to me."

Katrina was the scary Russian waitress who had once been on an Olympic shot put team. Or so people liked to say. I had no idea if it was true, but the girl was intimidating, and she scared the shit out of me.

Zeb laughed. "Yeah, she won't talk to you for the first

three months. Not until you prove that you're going to stick around."

As the restaurant closed, more of our co-workers trickled into the bar. Aaron, a bartender from Antonio's, pulled up a stool to the table Zeb and I were sitting at.

"How's it going, Tracksuit?" Zeb asked him.

"Worst nickname ever," Aaron said.

"Your fault, but seriously, I'm a fan of the last one—the white one with red piping. Where's Nat?" Zeb asked.

"She went home. Said she had a headache," Aaron answered.

I liked the staff. We were all around the same age bracket within five years. No one was married or tied down except for Jess, our GM, but she was cool—even if she was an adult.

I had never felt less like an adult.

Aidan sauntered in, his button-down shirt open, revealing a white undershirt.

"Damn, he is hot," Zeb breathed.

"That seems to be the general consensus," I admitted.

"You don't think he's hot?"

"Not my type."

Lie, lie, big fat lie.

"I wouldn't mind a make-out sesh in the wine room with him," Zeb said.

"Ew. I'm eating here," Aaron grumbled.

"You might have to fight Natalie for him," I said. I suddenly had a vision of Natalie and Zeb using Italian sausages like swords and fighting gladiator style for Aidan.

"I can take that skinny Asian chick. And make Aidan question his sexuality."

"If anyone can make a man question his sexuality, it's you," I said.

Zeb brightened. "Thanks. That means a lot."

"I'm going to go over there now while you girls talk about cute boys," Aaron said, picking up his half-eaten burger and going to hang out with the kitchen guys at another table.

"How long has Aidan worked at Antonio's?" I asked.

"Two years," Zeb answered. "Did you know the place was kind of failing until he came along?"

"Really?"

Zeb nodded. "Julian was running shit into the ground. He thought because he was the chef, that meant he under-stood how the front of the house was supposed to be run. Aidan turned it all around, kept Julian contained in the kitchen. Guests love Aidan and server tips got so much better in general."

"Wow, so he's like a restaurant savant?"

"Pretty much. He never has to write anything down to remember it, and he's really good with numbers."

"Huh." I thought he was just the quintessential hot guy. Now that I realized there was more to him…

"He ever hook up with an employee?"

Zeb shook his head. "No, sadly. Not even a hostess."

"Does he have a girlfriend?"

"No." His eyes narrowed. "Why are you asking?"

Thankfully, Aidan came over and plopped down in an empty seat next to me, sparing me from having to come up with a bad lie. "Good job tonight," he said.

"Thanks."

"You held your own."

"Yeah, she did," Zeb said. He raised his glass, saying loudly, "To Sibby!"

"To Sibby!" our co-workers cheered.

"Where are you going?" Zeb demanded as I stood to leave. "We're just about to do shots!"

"I'm exhausted," I said, which was partially the truth.

I'd been drunk once around Aidan, and had barely held on to my willpower. I didn't want to risk being drunk around him again and giving in this time.

Zeb replied, "Wednesday night is my birthday. I'm having a party at Barcade. The one in Brooklyn. 8:00 p.m."

"Brooklyn, huh? I'll be there."

Chapter 6

Prosciutto [pro-shu-toh]:

    1. Cured ham (from the leg).

    2. "No Ma'am, it's not a vegetable, fish, beef, or kosher."

I was back at Antonio's on Tuesday, fully recovered after my first Saturday night. Natalie and I were in the courtyard room together, waiting for the night to start. We polished wine glasses as we watched a table of nine guys being sat at the long community table.

"I really don't want to take them," she said. They looked like they were about my age, and I wondered if it was a frat boy reunion—they were all dressed in khakis and blue button-downs, all looking the same. A pack of bros. I couldn't tell them apart if I wanted to.

Weird.

"Why not?" I asked.

"They just look like—well—"

"Frat-tastic?"

"Yeah."

"I'll take them."

"You will?"

I nodded. "I haven't taken a bigger party yet, and it's a slower night. I should learn, right? Besides, I speak frat boy. I got this."

After I brought the bros water, the alpha bro at the head of the table demanded, "I wanna order drinks."

"Sure," I said, pulling out my pad and pen.

"Four Kettle tonics, four Kettle on the rocks, and one sangria."

"Sangria?" I repeated.

"Yeah," Alpha Bro said.

"Sure, Bro, whatever you want." As I dropped off their drinks, I shamelessly listened to their conversation, not that they cared there was a female in their midst. If I had any doubt that they were frat guys, I didn't after hearing them talk about the women in their lives. People said the most personal things in restaurants, mistakenly thinking they were in a private setting. One bro was talking about hooking up with two women in the same night. His friend-bro elbowed him and then gestured to me with his chin.

"Sorry," the bro said, not at all contrite.

"It's cool. I did that with two guys last weekend. You ready to order?"

The table of nine bros blinked stupidly, not sure if I was serious or kidding. I let them wonder as I took their order: fried calamari and caprese salads for starters, followed by six chicken Parmesans, and three spaghetti and meatballs.

So original.

Sometime in the middle of their appetizers, they switched from discussing women to chatting about their stock portfolios. I wanted to bang my head against the brick wall of the courtyard, but I managed to restrain myself.

"Can you split the check nine ways?" Alpha Bro asked, gathering up nine credit cards.

I felt my left eyeball twitch. "Sure."

Thank God it wasn't busy. As they left, I gathered up their signed credit card slips, making sure I had all of them. I didn't want to have to forge their signatures.

"How did you do with your first big party?" Jess asked me after they left.

"Okay."

"How were they?"

"Bro-tastic. I had to listen to them objectify women and then discuss their investment portfolios. Oh, and then split the check nine ways since none of them actually have money to cover the bill. Jackasses, all of them." I looked at the receipts and sighed. "Damn it."

"What? Shitty tippers?"

"Just when I think their mothers would be completely ashamed of them, they prove me wrong. They all tipped twenty-five percent." I shook my head. "This is proof you can never judge a bro by his khakis."

"What beers do you have on draft?" the man asked.

"Pork Slap Pale Ale, Laguinitas IPA, Bittburger Pilsner, and Easy Blonde Ale."

"Well, I liked easy blondes before my wife, so I'll go with that."

I looked at the man's wife who was sitting across from her husband, smiling and shaking her head. I laughed. "You actually take him out in public?"

She chuckled. "I know, right?"

They reached across the table and held hands. If I were in a far less bitter place, I would consider telling them I thought they were super cute. But at the moment, all I wanted to do was throw things at happy people. It probably wouldn't help my tip if I beamed them with olives from the bar.

I dropped off their drinks and then took their order. After I gathered up their menus, I watched them gaze at each other with affectionate expressions.

I went to my next table of two young twenty-some-things, a couple seemingly on a date. I watched as the girl posted photos of the restaurant, the table, the guy she was with, and everything in between on Facebook, instead of talking to her boyfriend. I never realized how much time some people spent absorbed in their electronic devices.

"Y'all ready to order?" I asked.

The guy smiled, relieved to have someone to finally talk to. "Y'all? Where are you from?"

"Atlanta."

"I'd like to order," the girl snapped, looking up from her phone.

"Okay," I said, not at all letting her attitude affect me. It wasn't my fault her boyfriend liked my drawl.

"I'll have the Brussels sprouts, but I don't want them sweet."

"Okay. I can do those without the maple syrup."

"Good. And no butter. Only olive oil—and make sure they're crunchy. That's all," she said and went right back to her phone.

I nodded and then looked to the guy. He was gazing at me with a slight smile on his face. Pretty obvious he thought I was cute.

"For you, sir?" I asked.

"I'll have the salmon."

"Great. How would you like it cooked?"

"Huh?"

I blinked. "Your fish. How would you like it cooked?"

"Sorry, I zoned out. Medium rare please."

"Sure, I'll bring it out as soon as it's done."

When the time came, they split the check. No surprise: the girl left me an 8% tip, but the guy, he totally came through for me: 30% and a phone number.

Maybe next time she'd stay off her phone.

I was in the middle of frosting the homemade birthday cake I'd made for Zeb when my phone rang.

Mom.

I hadn't spoken to her or my father since I'd gotten laid off and broken up with Matt. I silenced the call. She left a voicemail, but I didn't listen to it. I'd call them back when I had a new life plan. It could be a while.

After I finished frosting the cake and managed to get frosting all over my shirt, I went to change for the night out. I was heading to a dive bar in Brooklyn that had old school video games, like PAC-MAN and Centipede for people to play, so it wasn't like I needed to wear heels or a skirt. Not that I would've worn that stuff anyway.

I wasn't good at the dressing-up-like-a-girl thing. Makeup was a nuisance, contacts were a hassle, and a flat iron—why singe perfectly good curly hair? My eyebrows were sculpted, and I shaved my legs and armpits. That was as good as it was going to get.

I knew my limitations.

Hating my line of thought, I cut it off immediately and put on a vintage Rolling Stones T-shirt, black skinny-leg jeans, and my well-loved red Converse sneakers.

I grabbed the aluminum covered cake and my purse and was out the door. I caught a cab easily, and since I was only going to Williamsburg and I lived in Greenpoint, I figured it was worth the cheap ride. Maneuvering public transit with a cake would've been a nightmare. I could've walked, but exercise wasn't my style.

I found my co-workers in the back of the bar. They were already loud and laughing, and I felt a smile drift across my face. Most of them had been at Antonio's for years, and even though I was new, I felt like I already fit in with them.

"You came!" Zeb yelled in excitement, raising his bottle of beer to me.

"I said I would." I set the cake down on a scarred wooden table. "Sorry I'm late. I had to make you a cake."

"You made me a cake?" he screamed in drunken excitement.

"It's your birthday, right? People get cakes on their birthdays."

Apparently, Zeb liked to drink on his birthday. He was already trashed and in the crook of Kirk's arm. Kirk was our weekend service bartender, a stoic guy who rarely said a thing. I guess he was cute in that silent kind of way.

"I'm gonna grab a drink. Need anything?"

Zeb gestured to his nearly full bottle of beer. "Nope. I'm good."

"What? You're not gonna offer to buy me a drink?" Aaron asked.

"I don't buy drinks for men who wear tracksuits," I teased.

"You haven't worked at Antonio's long enough to mock me," Aaron protested.

"Yes, she has," Zeb interjected with a grin.

While I waited to snag the bartender's attention, I felt a body press next to mine and turned to find Aidan leaning in close to me.

"Hello," he said.

"Hi," I said warily. "You just get here?"

"Yeah. Nice T-shirt."

"Thanks," I said. "I made Zeb a yellow cake with buttercream frosting."

"You might just be the perfect woman," Aidan said with a smile.

"None of that," I warned.

"None of what?"

"Flirting. We had a deal."

"We had no such deal. *You* said no flirting. *I* said nothing about flirting."

The bartender finally came to our aid and Aidan asked me, "What do you want to drink?"

"Oh, you don't have to—"

"Sibby. Drink," Aidan said.

I sighed. "Beer please, but nothing hoppy. I don't do IPAs."

"Two Blue Moons, please," Aidan said to the bartender. He turned his attention back to me. "Why are you so resistant to my charms?"

"You don't have charms," I stated.

"Yeah, right. You think I'm charming. Admit it."

"Never."

"Caleb still talks about Annie."

"Good for Caleb."

"Why doesn't she want to get involved with guys… aside from the biblical involvement?"

"That's not really any of your business," I said.

He shrugged, letting it go. "Wanna play Asteroids?"

"No, thanks."

"Natalie!" Aidan called, taking his beer and strolling towards our group. "Game of Asteroids?"

"Sure!" Natalie said, hopping up from her stool like an eager puppy at the promise of a dog treat. Maybe tonight would be the night she made a move on Aidan.

I was instantly jealous, which was stupid, because I didn't want Aidan. I didn't want him flirting with me, or smiling at me, or buying me beer.

I smacked my forehead.

In public.

"You okay?" Zeb asked, not moving out from underneath Kirk's arm. I wondered how much Zeb had had to drink since it looked like he and Kirk were headed to Make-Out Central.

"Fine."

I turned my head and caught Natalie tossing her long, black, hot Asian hair over her shoulder and laughing at something Aidan was saying. He leaned forward, looking conspiratorial. Conspiratorial and sexy.

Screw this, time to get wasted.

"I'm drunk," I muttered.

"Yeah, but you're a fun drunk," Zeb said as he took my hand and led me to the dance floor.

"No, I don't dance," I stated, trying to tug my arm free from his grasp.

"Come on, it's my birthday!"

"So what? That won't change the fact that I look like a drunken octopus when I dance."

"Show me!"

"No!"

"It will be your birthday gift to me."

"I already made you a cake!"

"Please?" he begged. "Please, please, please?"

"Fine." I stood in the center of the dance floor, planted my feet, and then began swinging my arms back and forth like limp noodles that resembled the tentacles on a sea creature. Zeb cracked up and I grinned.

"You're right, you do look like a drunken octopus."

"I think you're an awesome dancer," Tracksuit said.

"You just want in her pants," Zeb shot back.

Tracksuit shrugged and nodded.

"Don't fall for it," Zeb stage whispered to me. "He's a flirt."

"Aren't all bartenders?"

"Not all…" he said with a look at Kirk.

We continued to dance until Zeb broke off to make out with Kirk. I turned my back on Natalie and Aidan flirting, clutching my near empty beer glass and continuing to dance. I was probably making a fool of myself, but I didn't really care. My head was spinning and I suddenly wanted to be home and in bed. I stumbled towards the exit.

"Sibby, wait! I'll help you," Aidan called.

"I'm fine." I gulped in a breath of fresh air when I made it to the sidewalk.

"You almost left your purse." He stood next to me, holding out my bag.

"Thanks," I said, and tripped over my own two feet as I reached for it.

"Come on," he said, raising his arm to flag down a cab. One stopped almost immediately, and he opened the door for me. I climbed inside and he settled next to me.

"What are you doing?" I demanded.

"Making sure you get home okay," he said.

"Chivalrous. Thought all the men like you were gone."

"Where are we going?"

I gave the cabbie my address and leaned back and closed my eyes before immediately opening them. "You're not the kind of guy to just show up at your ex-girlfriend's apartment, are you?" I demanded.

"I need more information before I answer that."

I didn't smile at his teasing tone. "Matt showed up, slept in the hallway waiting for me to get home," I mumbled.

"Why?" Aidan wondered.

"I don't know," I said. "I think he wanted to talk about the guy he cheated on me with, and I *so* don't need to hear about that. Really. I always thought I was a smart girl, ya know? Choose a good guy and get a decent job. Turns out both ideas were crap. Great. Now I'm playing the victim card. The drunk victim card, no less."

The cab came to a stop and before I could find my credit card to pay, Aidan was handing over a few bills. "Chivalrous," I repeated. "Wanna come up?"

"Duh." Aidan said as he helped me out of the car.

"Not for that," I warned. "I'm not a drunk-hookup kind of girl, but if I were, it would definitely be with you."

"Thanks, I think."

"I just really don't—do you want to come up still?"

He shoved his hands into his pockets. "Yeah, I do."

We climbed the stairs and when we got to the fourth floor, I stopped abruptly causing Aidan to bump into me. Matt was sitting on the floor, doing something on his phone, waiting for me.

Again.

"What the fuck are you doing here?" I demanded.

"Are you drunk?" Matt scrambled up from his place on the floor.

"It's a strong possibility."

Matt's eyes slid to the man behind me. "Who are you?"

Before Aidan could reply, my drunken mouth ran away from me and blurted, "Your replacement."

God bless Aidan, he didn't pause when he moved to my side and wrapped an arm around me in a protective gesture.

"What? You can hook up with a guy, but I can't?" I asked.

"Will you just freakin' talk to me?" Matt begged. "I didn't mean for it to end the way it did."

"You've been haunting my hallway to say something that generic? I can't believe I wasted two years on you. Come on, Aidan, let's go inside and have hot monkey sex. And do that thing with your hips that I really like."

"You got it, babe." Aidan smirked.

I had the pleasure of watching Matt's face pale. He moved out of the way while I got my keys out of my bag. "Sibby," he began.

"It's fine, Matt. It's all fine, okay? We're so good. You have Taylor and I have Aidan. Take care of yourself."

"Please," Matt pleaded. "Can we have coffee? I really want to explain."

"You don't have to. I know what I walked in on." I glowered. "The image is blurred into my brain."

Matt blinked. "I think you mean *burned*."

"What the fuck ever," I scoffed. "Seriously. Don't keep loitering in the hallway."

"Then promise me coffee. Not now, or tomorrow, but sometime in the future."

"Fine. I'll call you."

Matt held my gaze a long moment and then nodded. He glanced at Aidan and said softly, "Take care of her," before heading down the stairs.

"Are you really going to have coffee with him?"

I sighed, unlocking the front door. "I don't know. I just wanted him to leave."

"He doesn't look like I thought he'd look," Aidan said, taking a seat at the kitchen table. I opened the fridge and pulled out the covered mixing bowl of leftover frosting and set it down in front of him.

I frowned. "How did you think he'd look?"

"I don't know. I pictured you with a really huge guy with no neck."

"Very specific," I said with a grin.

He paused. "You okay?"

I blew out a breath of air, stirring my bangs. "Yeah, think so."

"He seems to care about you," Aidan pointed out.

"I hope you're wrong about that. Because if he is concerned, it makes him more human and less douchebag."

He laughed. "I really like you, Sibby."

I inhaled a shaky breath. "I like you, too, Aidan. You're a good spooner. Did you know that?"

"I've been told."

"I know it's not the same, you know, sleeping in bed with a girl and not getting any action, but—I'm just drunk and vulnerable enough to ask—will you spoon me tonight?" I looked at him.

"Depends," he said slowly.

"On?"

He grinned. "Can I have the rest of that frosting?"

"Fine, but no inappropriate sexual frosting comments, okay?"

"Do I look like the kind of guy that would make inappropriate frosting comments?"

"Yes."

He sighed. "You already know me so well."

Chapter 7

Biscotti [bee-skoh-tee]

   1. Small, crisp rectangular, twice-baked cookie, typically containing nuts. Made originally in Italy.

   2. Hard, flavorless cookie that someone left in the oven too long and thought, "I wonder if I can still sell this?"

   I sat up in bed, wincing at the dreamy daylight coming in through the curtains. I looked over at Aidan, whose eyes were sleepy but open. They watched me, unnerved me, and I struggled to find something witty to say.

   "We have to stop spooning like this," I blurted out.

His smile was better than the sun coming out from behind the clouds on a cold winter day.

"I know you can do better than that."

I shook my head, fighting a smile. "I feel like my brain is just sitting in a vat of hops, slushing around in there. I've had more to drink in the last few weeks than I've had in the last two years."

Aidan ran a hand through his dark bed head. "Industry people drink and party. At least no one at Antonio's does coke. I worked at a club once—"

"Wouldn't it just be easier to stick my liver in a bottle of tequila and call it a day? I don't think I'm cut out for it. This is a surefire way to never find my direction, and lose brain cells in the process."

"You're chattering like a monkey. You okay?"

"Nervous," I admitted. "Nervous and hungover."

"Greasy diner food is a known cure for both."

"You ever been to Peter Pan?"

"Huh?" Aidan asked.

"It's a bakery."

"Oh. No, I haven't."

"We have to change this. Pants. Immediately."

"Aye, aye, Captain."

I headed to the bathroom to brush my teeth when Aidan popped his head in.

"Can I get a little of that?" he asked, holding out his pointer finger. I doused it with toothpaste, and we brushed in silence. My nerves were straightening out. I handed him a towel to dry his face and he took it with a grin.

When we were headed to Peter Pan, Aidan asked, "So, was this morning easier to handle than last time?"

"Easier? Maybe."

He laughed. "You can spoon me anytime you want."

"I didn't spoon you, you spooned me, remember?"

"Oh, I remember."

I made an embarrassed noise in the back of my throat as I pulled open the bright green door of the bakery. There was a line for takeout orders, but there were two vacant stools at the counter for dining in.

"You have to be quick," I said, dodging to the counter. We plopped down and I watched Aidan take it all in, from the smell of fried dough to the Polish waitresses in classic turquoise waitress uniforms. The place looked like it had been frozen in 1955.

A young pixieish waitress approached us and set down two paper napkins. Aidan looked at me. "What should I get?"

I smiled. "I got this. Two coffees please, and two bacon, egg, and cheese on everything bagels."

"Toasted?" the waitress asked in a thick Polish accent.

"Yes please, and also one Bavarian cream éclair and one red velvet donut." The waitress left in a blur.

"That was some ordering," Aidan said.

"Just wait. Do you want orange juice?" I asked, hopping up off the stool and heading to the small glass refrigerator in the back corner.

"Yeah. Thanks."

I handed him the OJ and he stuck his straw into it and took a sip. "God, what is it about OJ when you're hungover?"

"Nutrient deficiency and dehydration," I answered.

The waitress set down our coffees, donut, and éclair and then went to deal with more customers. I watched Aidan take a bite of the éclair, licking the Bavarian cream from his top lip.

"Holy shit," he said.

"Your life will never be the same again," I muttered, no longer thinking about my hangover or the donuts.

He grinned, his dark hair messy, crumbs falling onto his shirt. "No, I don't think it will be."

"Thanks for breakfast," Aidan said as we stood on the street.

"Thanks for making sure I got home okay last night."

"You going to thank me for staying, too? And for using me as your teddy bear?" he prodded.

"I will not. That would make it sound like I needed you—and I don't need you."

He grinned. "Okay, Prickly Pear."

"Don't call me that."

He laughed. "Admit it. You like hanging out with me."

"I will admit no such thing."

"I'm so gonna wear you down."

"Bye, Aidan," I said, giving him a little push towards the subway.

"Bye, Sibby."

I watched him walk away, wondering why I enjoyed the way his hair flopped in the breeze. I took out my phone and called Annie.

"Hello?" she said.

"I absolutely refuse to have feelings for Aidan."

She paused. "What did you do?"

I told her about my night.

"That's not that bad," she said when I was finished.

"It's not that good, either," I said.

"So, stay away from him."

"I'm trying," I said weakly. "But I do work with the guy."

She snorted with laughter.

"What are you doing?" I asked.

"Talking you off a ledge, obviously."

"You wanna hang out?"

"Can't. Some of us have to work during the day."

"I'm pretty sure you just called me lazy. And a vampire. A lazy vampire."

"Vampires are overrated."

I stood in line at the coffee shop and it took all of my will power not to laugh when I heard the hipster girl in front of me order a free trade, half-caff, sugar-free hazelnut, no foam, skim latte. When Hipster Girl reached for her concoction, she chirped out a *thanks!* and didn't bother leaving a tip.

"What can I get you?" asked the harassed barista as I stepped up to the counter.

"Just a plain old black coffee," I said.

"I love you," the barista muttered. I paid for my coffee and dropped a few bucks in the tip jar. I didn't want to worry about my karma.

Winding my way through the coffee shop, I parked it

across the table from Zeb. We were a block away from work and had an hour to kill. I hadn't seen him since his birthday a few days before, and when he texted asking if I wanted to grab a cup of coffee, I said yes. It was nice feeling like I was making some real friends. Hanging outside of work with work people was a change from the office gig, where everyone kept to themselves, didn't talk about personal stuff and went home to their tiny apartments and unhappy marriages.

"So are you going to tell me about you and Kirk?"

He grinned. "We ate the rest of the cake you made for breakfast."

"Glad it went over well," I teased. "The cake, I mean."

"Kirk doesn't say a lot, and I'm starting to think that might be a necessary quality in future boyfriends. Or at least future hook up buddies."

We laughed.

"So, sleeping with someone you work with…you're not worried about people knowing?"

He shrugged. "I mean, maybe, but there's an end in sight to working at Antonio's. I finally declared a major."

"Really?"

"Yeah. I can't be a perpetual student."

"What's your major?"

"Communications."

Communications. Also known as, *undecided about life*.

"Wow," I said. "Congratulations."

"Thank you."

"So…Kirk?"

"Not the kind of guy to make it weird."

"Because he doesn't talk a lot."

"Exactly."

"Will there be a repeat performance?" I asked.

"There already has been," Zeb said, waggling his

eyebrows. "It's hard to date when you work in a restaurant. Our hours are whacked; the only other people who work similar hours are our fellow co-workers, or strippers."

"Don't date a stripper."

"Been there, done that. It wasn't pretty."

"Wow, you've lived so much," I said.

"Girl…" He shook his head. "So, did you go home with Aidan?"

I choked on my coffee and a bit of it went right up my nose. "What? No. He put me in a cab and then went home."

He studied me for a moment. "Okay."

"Okay? What do you mean, okay?"

"I mean, okay. Just for the record—you can't keep secrets in a restaurant. You hook up with someone, everyone knows. And I mean everyone from the dishwasher to the absent owner."

"Why? How?"

"Restaurant life bleeds over into real life. Waiting tables is like war. Your co-workers are there with you in the trenches, you get close."

"Are you sure you're not a theater major? You sound pretty dramatic."

"I'm gay."

"Same thing."

Zeb didn't smile. "No secrets."

"You mean people aren't trustworthy?"

"I mean, things always have a way of coming out. So don't do anything that you wouldn't want the entire staff knowing."

I became exasperated. "There's nothing coming out. Nothing happened with Aidan. He's a good guy who made sure I got home okay."

"I saw the way you looked at him the night of my party."

"What way was that?" I demanded.

"Like he was a plate of duck fat fries."

Yum.

The fries, I meant.

"But I also noticed how he looked at you."

A stupid girly excited thrill shot through me. "You were drunk. You don't know what you saw."

He shrugged. "Denial is good."

"I'm not denying anything!"

"Whatever you say."

"Can we go to work now, please?"

I slid along the slippery kitchen floor, nearly losing my balance as I dropped off a pile of dishes to the dishwasher. The guys behind the line threw dirty pots into crates; the dishwashers collected them and all but tossed them into the massive sinks. The clatter of plates and silverware was downright jarring, and I was still adjusting to the noise level of the restaurant. Working in an office setting had been so quiet. The hum of computers and low phone conversations was all anyone ever heard.

But a restaurant?

Oy.

All the people. So. Many. People. All the time, all

around. Bumping into customers, tight service stations with co-workers. I wasn't used to having so many people in my space—not four nights a week. It was a lot to process.

I was headed out of the kitchen when the French chef, Julian, stopped me by placing his big, burly body in front of me. I nearly ran into him and his starched white chef coat.

"Ah!" I yelped and jumped back.

"You selling fish?" he asked.

I nodded.

"How much?"

I blinked. "Uhm, couple of branzino. A salmon or two—"

"Tuna!" he barked. "How many tuna?"

I tried not to quake. Julian was intimidating. "No tuna. Not yet."

"Sell tuna, or you be sleeping with the zucchini." His eyes bored into mine.

"Sleeping with the *zucchini?*" I murmured in confusion.

Julian didn't blink. He looked like an enraged bull. His face was red, and I was convinced he was about to have an apoplectic fit at any moment. "Sleeping. With. The. Zucchini."

"Okay, I understand," I said even though I didn't. I scurried out of the kitchen. At least he hadn't thrown a plate at me to get his point across.

I approached the couple who had set their menus aside and were conversing over their bottle of wine.

"Any questions about the menu?" I asked.

The middle-aged woman looked at me. "How's the tuna?"

"So good," I stated quickly.

"Really?"

"Really."

"You wouldn't just be saying that, would you?" the gentleman asked.

I pointed to my face. "Does this look like the face of a liar?"

The gentleman smiled. "In that case, we'll both have the tuna."

I collected the menus and breathed a quiet sigh of relief. Tonight, at least, I wouldn't be sleeping with the zucchini.

I stared at the fake-tanned woman holding the check. She was Oompa Loompa orange. Gesturing with her hands, her face was screwed up like an infant who hadn't gotten its way and was about to cry big fat snotty tears.

"This is outrageous," she continued. "I'm not paying for the pasta."

"I don't understand," I said in confusion.

"The pasta was terrible." She raised her eyebrows as she waited for my response. Her friend sitting across from her hid her face like she was ashamed to be out to dinner with such a *kvetcher*. And yet, she wouldn't rein in her friend.

"But—"

"I demand to speak to your manager."

I nodded. "Okay." I headed to the host stand where

Aidan was changing out the grimy dessert menus. "I have a problem."

"Animal, vegetable, mineral?"

"Animal."

"Julian? I heard him giving you a hard time about tuna."

"Not Julian," I said. "Angry customer. She said she's not paying for the pasta."

"Did she say what was wrong with it?"

"Wrong? She ate the entire dish."

"Is there anything left in the bowl?"

"No."

"Did she try to send it back before now?"

"No."

"You're kidding."

"Oh, I wish that I was."

"I'll handle it."

I grinned. "You're the best. All hail The King."

"I like the sound of that."

He was sexy when he was in crisis solving mode.

"What table?"

"Twenty-three."

"Stay out of sight," he said.

"Roger that."

I hid in the service station by the bar, but I had a view that allowed me to see and hear the table. Aidan held the empty plate in his hand, nodding at Oompa Loompa.

"I understand that, ma'am," he said with just enough deference to make me wonder how he did this job without going homicidal on someone. Maybe he was just even-keeled. I was beginning to think that I wasn't really a people person. In fact, I believed working in the service industry was giving me a social anxiety disorder.

Oompa Loompa snapped, "But the dish was terrible!"

"Ma'am," Aidan cut her off, "this is a restaurant. We would have been glad to bring you something else if only you had told us you didn't like it. But you ate the entire dish. There's nothing left. You ate it, you bought it."

The women dug around in their purses and threw down cash, grabbing their belongings and muttering on the way out. Aidan picked up the cash and brought it to me.

"I didn't get a tip, did I?" I asked.

He looked sheepish. "Nope."

"Totally worth it," I said with a grin.

"How is everything?" I asked the table of four.

I received a lot of head nods and thumbs up because everyone was still chewing. It was better than verbal confirmation. One guy dabbed his mouth with his napkin before looking up at me.

"What bourbons do you have?"

"Maker's, Knob Creek, Jim Beam, Jim Beam Rye, Jack, Gentleman Jack, Woodford Reserve, Michter's, George Dickel, Bulleit and Bulleit Rye."

"No Wild Turkey?"

"No Wild Turkey."

"Why not?"

My brow furrowed. "What do you mean?"

"I mean, you have almost every other bourbon under the sun, but you don't have Wild Turkey?"

I didn't know how to respond, so I stayed silent.

Bourbon Guy clearly wasn't finished as he went on, "Can you get me Wild Turkey? I just want Wild Turkey on the rocks."

"Uhm—"

"I saw a liquor store down the street. Can't you just pop over there and get me a mini bottle?"

"I can't leave the restaurant, sir." The dining room was full, and we were in a middle of our rush. "But I'll be glad to get you something else from our bar."

"I don't want anything else," he huffed, acting like a child, picking up his fork and shoveling in another bite of food.

"Okay," I said meekly, skulking away. I headed towards the bar, wanting to hide from the angry customer.

"What's wrong?" Zeb asked when he came over to pick up his drinks.

I told him about Bourbon Guy. Zeb rolled his eyes and called out to Kirk behind the bar. "Gimme a shot of Maker's."

"What are you doing?" I asked.

"I'm telling him we found a rogue bottle of Wild Turkey. Ten bucks says that guy won't know the difference." He stalked toward my table, carrying Maker's on the rocks. Thirty seconds later, Zeb was back, grinning in triumph.

"Pay up," he said.

Chapter 8

Saltimbocca [sal-tim-boh-ka]

    1. Veal wrapped in prosciutto and sage. Literally means *jumps in the mouth* because it's so good.

    2. Jump into my belly. Now.

    The next night, I was folding a stack of napkins when Jess, the GM, came into the dining room holding a clipboard. "Sibby, can you come here for a second?"

    I set a folded napkin aside. "I didn't do it."

    "Do what?" she asked.

    "Whatever it is you want to accuse me of," I teased.

    "You're not in trouble."

I followed her into the semi-private room that sat ten—twelve, if the guests were skinny girls. I sat in the booth and stared at her. "What's up?"

"You've been here a little over a month and I just wanted to check in with you."

"Oh, my review, huh?"

Jess smiled. "Something like that. You seem to be doing okay. Fitting in?"

I nodded. "The staff is really great. Katrina still won't talk to me, but I'm not taking it personally."

"You shouldn't. She was here before me, and she didn't speak to me for three months."

"That's reassuring."

"Julian has nice things to say about you."

I raised my eyebrows. "The chef has nice things to say about me?"

"Okay, nice is too generous a word. More like, he doesn't want to wring your neck like a chicken. Your tip average is good, your check average is good."

"So, everything is good."

"Everything is good."

"One question," I said.

"Shoot."

"The kitchen guys call me *flakita*. Any idea what that means? I don't speak Spanish."

Jess laughed. "Yeah, I have an idea."

"Am I going to be offended?"

"Maybe. *Flakita* means little skinny."

"Little skinny? Like, I'm not one or the other, I'm both?"

She smirked. "Are they flirting with you?"

"Yes."

"Are they giving you free food?"

I squirmed. "Yes. Cookies, mostly. Though, now that I

88

think about it, it's probably because they think I'm too freakin' skinny."

Our meeting ended and I headed back to the floor. Only two tables had been seated during my brief meeting and Zeb had taken both of them. Antonio's was a pooled house, so it didn't matter what section the customers sat in, we all got a share in the tips. We were all team players. *Team player* was thrown out a lot at Antonio's.

"Slow start today," I commented.

Zeb nodded. "Yep. And you know what Jess says when it's slow? If you have time to lean, you have time to clean. Oh, and fold napkins."

"I'll make a napkin fort," I promised. "Want to play a game?"

"Totally."

"Can you speak in an accent?"

"A Midwestern one."

I grinned. "I'll raise you a Midwestern accent with a British one. And if you speak in the accent to your tables, I'll buy drinks at Johnny's tonight."

"You're on."

"Hi, how are you?" I asked, as I approached the lone chubby man at the table.

"Diet coke," he replied without glancing at me.

I paused, waiting for him to get off his Blackberry to look at me. Finally, he stopped staring at his phone.

"Should we try that again?" I asked.

Chubster raised his eyebrows, appearing surprised.

"Hi, how are you?"

"Uhm. Good? You?"

I smiled sincerely. "I'm great. Thanks so much for asking. Can I get you something to drink?"

"Diet Coke. Please," he added.

"Absolutely."

I turned and nearly danced towards the bar. "Did you just do what I think you did?" Zeb asked.

"What do you think I did?"

"You corrected that guy's manners."

"Yep."

"But you—he—"

I smiled at him. "You're in awe of me right now, aren't you?"

He nodded. "You get away with murder. I think it's because you're small and cute. Like a little woodland creature. You can't be mad at a little woodland creature."

"Yeah, but customers think you're hilarious when you're being Queen Bitch. They have no idea you're actually judging them."

"Yeah, well, people are stupid."

After a quick drink at Johnny's, I trudged home. The night had started off slow without promise, but then the customers came like a swarm of locusts and I'd been running for three hours. The smell of hot oil and fried shrimp hit my nose, and I wondered what my neighbors were cooking. And then I realized it came from me.

My clothing was saturated with the stench.

I liked my co-workers and the money, but did I have to smell like a deep fryer?

Stripping out of my clothes, I headed for the bathroom. I showered quickly, donned a pair of pajamas, and was in the process of looking through the fridge for food when my buzzer sounded.

It was 11:00 p.m. on a Thursday night. I hoped it wasn't Matt.

The buzzer buzzed again.

"Hello?" I said through the intercom.

"It's Aidan."

"What are you doing here?" I said.

"Can I come up?" he asked without answering my question.

I bit my lip. I hadn't seen him at the restaurant for a few days—he'd been off. Sighing, knowing I'd regret it, but really wanting to see his smile, I buzzed him up.

I opened the door, only then realizing I was still in my matching, juvenile pajamas. They were comfortable, and I didn't care that they were pink cotton with a Care Bears pattern.

But now, my manager–slash–sometimes spooner was seeing me in them.

The shame. Oh, the shame.

"Nice jammies," Aidan said, leaning against the doorway, dressed in faded jeans and a white t-shirt.

I crossed my arms over my chest. "I wasn't expecting company. Why are you here?"

"I was in the neighborhood."

"I could've been at work."

"I make your schedule."

"That's creepy."

He laughed.

"Well, I feel a little better about the stalking thing. I could've been at Johnny's with Zeb."

"I took a chance." He sighed like he was tired. "You gonna let me in, or what?"

"What will you give me?"

"Chinese food."

"Chinese sucks."

"Then Thai."

I moved out of the way and let him in. "Wine?"

"Sure, thanks." He plopped down on the couch.

I got out a corkscrew and opened a bottle of Trader Joe's two-buck chuck.

"That's your idea of wine? I'm offended."

"Sorry," I said. "But it gets the job done." I handed him a glass. "Were you really in the neighborhood?"

"Sort of. I was in Williamsburg."

"Ew, why?"

Williamsburg was Hipsterville, USA.

Then I remembered *I* was a hipster—but at least I lived in Greenpoint.

"Caleb and I were at a friend's bar. Newly opened. We went to show our support."

"That was nice of you." I sat next to him and took a sip of my wine. "How is Caleb?"

"Still talking about Annie. He took a vow of celibacy."

"I don't believe that."

"Believe it."

"He's quite pathetic, isn't he?"

"Very," Aidan agreed. "Come on, you have to help me help him. We should trap them in an elevator together."

"That is a purely romantic comedy moment—and Annie hates romantic comedies. She's been known to watch them on mute and make up her own version of how things go."

"That actually sounds fun."

"It is. Especially when we've been drinking."

He smiled. "Should we go ahead and order food?"

"Thai placed closed half an hour ago," I said.

"And you let me in anyway? Interesting…"

"Drink your wine," I said. "I'll heat up leftovers."

"Leftovers?"

I grinned. "Annie came over the other day and made meatloaf and mashed potatoes. You know, if I was smart, I'd marry her and be done with it. We'd get tax breaks and I'd get good food."

"There's an idea."

"I'm hanging out with Annie next week. Monday night. Probably somewhere in your neck of the woods. If I text you, you and Caleb can casually run into us."

"You're crafty."

"The craftiest," I agreed. "You can't sleep over."

"Not this again," Aidan groaned.

"The last few times we've spooned I was drunk. It didn't count. I don't plan on getting hammered, so spooning is out of the question."

"Sober spooning is better than drunk spooning."

"You're just saying that."

"I'm really not. Sober spooning with me will change your life. Not as much as sober sex, but I'm willing to go at your speed."

"You're either really charming or really sincere."

"Am I wearing you down?"

I sighed. "Totally. You can stay."

"You're really hot," Aidan said.

I blinked and looked down at my pink pajamas.

"Okay," he amended, "well, maybe not at *this* moment, but you're hot. I thought you were hot the night we met."

"Yeah, a hot mess," I interjected.

"You're funny and weird, and I like that you have no idea what you want out of life."

"That's a little much, don't you think? I have a direction. Sort of."

He grinned. "It's okay, Sibby."

"What is?" I demanded. "What's okay? The fact that my life is a complete and utter mess? The fact that I walked in on my boyfriend of two years having sex with a man?"

I jumped up from the couch and began to pace across the living room carpet. "And on the day I caught my ex cheating on me, I was also laid off from the boringest job in the history of jobs."

"I doubt it was the boringest," Aidan interjected. "What about accounting? That seems way worse. Is boringest even a word?"

"I was a theater major," I ranted. "A playwright. And what did I do with it? Nothing. Absolutely nothing. Fuck!

94

My life is a joke! I've been avoiding my parents' phone calls because I don't have the heart to tell them that I'm single, got laid off, and now work in a restaurant."

"What's wrong with being single?"

"My mom will bring up the idea of freezing my eggs."

"She will not." Pause. "Really?"

I nodded.

"Oooookay. I'm just going to sail right past that. The laid off thing. That happens. And there's nothing wrong with working in a restaurant," Aidan pointed out while pointing to himself.

"Dad always said to use your mind, not your body to make a living."

"Was he talking about prostitution?"

"Stop joking."

"No," he said. "You take yourself way too seriously."

"Look at my pajamas! Do I look like I take myself too seriously?" I glared at Aidan, who attempted not to smile. He gave in and laughed, and eventually, so did I.

"Come here," he said softly.

I glanced at him, completely wary. I had very little willpower left, and Aidan was hot. Not to mention sweet, and a good listener. "I feel like I should blog."

"Blog?"

"Yeah, you know, take to the internet. Share my humiliation with the world. Maybe I can get people to lose a few calories over their breakfast."

"Sibby, come here," he said again. I clutched the hem of my shirt and blew out a puff of air. I went to him and then collapsed onto the couch. Curling into him, I let him put his arm around me. It was nice, comfortable, and yet it made my heart pound and my stomach do some sort of weird romance novel flippy thing.

"You don't have to have life all figured out. In fact, I

plan to never have it fully figured out. That's what keeps it fun."

He settled back against the couch, keeping his arm around me.

"Wanna watch TV?" I asked. "I could really go for a thirty-minute sitcom where everything gets resolved by the end."

"Ah, then you want to watch *Leave it to Beaver*."

"I'm starting to think you really get me."

"Any chance pearls and 1950s family dynamics get you all hot and bothered?" Aidan asked with a hopeful smile.

I woke up not being spooned. You can't really be spooned when you're sleeping half on top of the other person. Aidan didn't seem to mind.

And I didn't mind either.

I disentangled myself from him and went to brush my teeth. Though I believed in the power of the cute matching pajamas, I had no illusions about my morning breath.

After I brushed my teeth and put on the coffee, I checked my phone. There was one voicemail from my mother. I'd been avoiding my parents like the plague. A dramatic, Jewish plague that was overly invasive in my life.

I was gutless.

Knowing they at least needed to hear my voice, so they

didn't do something crazy like fly up to New York to check on me, I called her back.

"Hi, Mob," I answered, feigning a stuffy nose.

"What's wrong? Are you sick?"

"Yeah. Head cold."

"Aw, poor thing."

"I feel pretty terrible. My head feels like a bowling ball. I was just getting ready to curl up on the couch and take a nap."

"Is Matt taking care of you?"

"He's at work, Mob. Wish you were here. Your chicken noodle soup always makes me feel better. Lobe you."

"You sound terrible. Go to bed, I'll talk to you later. Love you, feel better."

I hung up, set my phone on the coffee table, and ran a hand though my hair.

"Wouldn't it just be easier to tell her the truth?" Aidan asked.

I jumped at the sound of his voice. "Jeez. Make a noise, would you?" He was in his shirt and boxers and he looked pretty delectable, even to a fake sick person. "I can't tell her the truth."

"Why not?"

"Because I know how the conversation would go. I'll give you a clue; it ends with me on anti-anxiety meds."

"Would you tell them about me?"

I rolled my eyes. "You should go."

He grinned. "Oooooh, am I one of your dirty little secrets?"

"Nothing dirty about our relationship."

"And whose fault is that?" he demanded. "I've been trying to make it dirty and you won't let me."

"Don't you have things to do today?"

"You're so harsh," he said, feigning hurt. "Fine, I'll go. See ya at work tonight?"

I nodded. "Unless I call out due to severe emotional sickness." I felt guilty for kicking him out, so I filled a to-go thermos of coffee and gave it to him.

"Thanks," he said in surprise. "You'd make a good girlfriend."

"You're giving me hives." I herded him towards the door and opened it. "I want that cup back!" I called after him.

Chapter 9

Taleggio [tah-leh-jee-oh]:
 1. A sweet creamy cow's milk cheese, pungent in odor.
 2. Smells like feet, but tastes delicious.

Jess walked into the dining room and took a seat on an empty bar stool. She set her clipboard of manager duties on the bar and passed out our special sheets which had about fifteen items listed, and they were always the same. Daily specials were supposed to change, but this was Antonio's, the place where logic went to die, or so Zeb liked to remind me on a regular basis.

"The owner wants to change some things up."

"Mutiny!" Zeb yelled. "No change!"

Jess rolled her eyes. "You don't even know what the change is."

"Let me guess. We're becoming a sports bar."

"No."

"We're going to start doing happy hour."

"No."

"We're—"

"New uniforms," Jess interrupted.

"But why? We've had six uniform changes in the past year. Should I go over them?"

"No need," Jess said, but Zeb acted like he hadn't heard.

"First, it was all black. Anything all black. Then it was jeans and gray shirts, but everyone wore different shades of gray, so it switched to jeans and black polos. Then jeans and the Antonio's T-shirt. Then black pants and gray button-downs. Then black pants and black button-downs. I'm not spending any more money on new uniforms! Stop the madness!" Zeb yelled.

"You done?" Jess asked.

Zeb took a deep breath. "For now."

"Black pants, white button-downs. The owner is paying for the shirts since he wants everyone to look the same."

"No black bowties?" Zeb demanded.

Jess grinned. "Not yet."

"I'm going to have to buy a white undershirt. Otherwise, customers will see my nipples." He stage whispered to me, "They're pierced."

"Might help increase your tips," I said with a shrug. "Can I see?"

He went to unbutton his shirt when Jess yelled, "For the love of God! Not at work!"

"Whatever, Jess, you're just jealous of my amazing nipples."

First night in my white button-down uniform and already it was covered in marinara sauce.

Braveheart extra, part two.

"How do you do it?" Aidan asked, trying not to laugh.

"Just my usual MO."

"Nice to have things you can count on."

"Well, you can always count on me for a laugh," I said with a hokey grin. "Now, if you'll excuse me, there are customers waiting to make me feel bad about myself."

"Do I want the duck?" the man at my table asked, taking in my appearance but generously not saying anything.

"Yes."

"How do I want it cooked?"

"Medium rare."

"You know what, you've got kind eyes. I trust you."

I pointed to my shirt. "You feel bad for me, don't you?"

"Perhaps."

"Please show it on the tip line," I said with a playful wink, causing him to laugh. I gathered the menus up and handed them off to a hostess as I headed to the computer station.

"Going strong with that no filter thing, huh?" Nat asked.

"Yeah, I'm a little too proud of myself."

"You're on a good streak."

"Thanks. I'm glad someone appreciates it."

"We *all* appreciate it. I'm really glad you came to work here."

"Oh," I said, pretending to get all *verklempt*. "If I had a heart, I would be moved to tears."

"I don't see linguine with clam sauce on the menu," the guy said.

"That's because we don't serve it," I stated.

"Why not?"

"Because the chef doesn't make it."

"But you're an Italian restaurant."

"Yeah," I nodded. "And we have a lot of other fine Italian dishes."

"Like fettuccine chicken Alfredo?" he asked hopefully.

Dear God.

"No, no fettuccini chicken Alfredo." Clearly the only Italian restaurant this guy had ever been to was Olive Garden.

"I don't know what to get," the guy complained. "You have nothing I want to eat!"

"Sir, our menu is huge. There must be something you

want that we have. We have spaghetti and meatballs, or chicken parm…" My voice trailed off as he shook his head.

"No, no, no! I don't want any of those things!"

"You should try our spaghetti Carbonara. It's fantastic; we're known for it."

"Really?" he asked, appearing intrigued. "Tell me about it."

"Three types of bacon with spaghetti, topped off with a poached egg. You mix the egg yolk as the sauce," I explained. "And then there's Parmesan cheese and fresh cracked black pepper."

"Hmmm…sounds interesting. Can I get it without the pork and add tomato sauce?"

Oy.

Monday night Annie and I sat on two bar stools in a wine bar on the Upper East Side. We were sharing a cheese plate and a bottle of wine. I was trying not to glance at the door every five minutes while I waited for Aidan and Caleb to show up. Our plan to get Annie and Caleb together was in motion.

"I can't believe you chose this place," Annie said. "And I can't believe you suggested we wear our little black dresses and heels."

"Just wanted to do something different."

"I like this," she said.

We toasted and I took another sip before I said, "Okay. I think I'm buzzed enough to admit something to you."

"Ready. Go!"

"I haven't had sex in eight months."

Annie blinked. "Come again?"

"I'm trying! Believe me!"

"Eight months? What the hell? You should've dumped Matt ages ago."

"Okay it's not completely true. We did get drunk a couple of months ago and have mediocre sex, but I don't think it really counts."

"It was probably his last foray in Straightsville before he bought a one-way ticket to Gaytown."

"Probably," I agreed. "I'm going crazy. I can't think straight. I kind of want to jump Aidan."

"Do it."

"We work together."

"So? That's a flimsy excuse."

It was—not to mention the fact that I just didn't care anymore. And I was hornier than a horny toad.

The man I wanted to have an animal kingdom wildlife moment with walked in, his best friend by his side. Caleb was attractive, too. They both were handsome and tall, but Caleb had light hair and Aidan had dark.

"Sibby!" Aidan exclaimed, widening his eyes in pretend shock. Annie's head whipped around, her gaze landing on Caleb.

"Aidan! This is so random!" I winced as I heard the insincerity of my tone.

I was a terrible actress.

"Hi," Caleb greeted, unable to take his eyes off Annie. Man, she must've done some crazy acrobatics in the bedroom. He looked like he was ready to get on his knees and worship her.

"Caleb," she said. She sounded breathless and though the lighting was low, I thought I could detect a faint blush on her cheeks. No one made Annie blush. No one.

Interesting.

"Buy you a drink?" Caleb asked.

She leaned over and whispered something in his ear that had him swallowing like a man dying of thirst. He nodded eagerly. Annie took her purse and looked at me. "Breakfast tomorrow."

"You got it."

Annie glanced at Caleb and then amended the offer. "Better make it lunch." She hopped off her stool and she and Caleb nearly ran from the bar.

Aidan took the available spot and grinned at me. "That worked out better than I could have hoped for."

I finished my glass of wine in three long swallows before I said, "I'd like to discuss something with you."

"Discuss away."

"Sex. You and me."

Aidan raised an eyebrow. "My, you are quite the romantic."

"I haven't had sex in eight months," I blurted out.

Long pause.

"Grab your purse," he said.

105

"Sibby," Aidan said.

"Hmm?"

"Sibby, remove your arm from your eyes."

"No," I said.

"Why not?"

"This is not good."

"On the contrary, I thought it was very good. Great in fact."

I finally lifted my arm from my eyes and glared at him. He was grinning like an idiot. A cute idiot with messed-up hair. A sheet covered his naked body. In my bed.

Hot.

"You're supposed to be tall, dark, and brooding," I said. "Not tall, dark, and witty."

"Okay, it's time for you to admit it. You like me. And not just for the sex, which would be enough in its own right. I'm a god."

"It *had* been eight months," I reminded him. "I'm thinking a high-school virgin could have gotten the job done."

"Good thing I have a healthy ego. That would've crushed a lesser man."

"I knew this was going to be a mistake," I said, finally getting out of bed and looking for my dress on the floor. Then I remembered I'd lost it somewhere in the living room. The moment we'd gotten back to the privacy of my apartment, I'd climbed Aidan like a koala climbed a tree.

I was a naked koala.

I hastily opened my dresser and pulled on a t-shirt. "I've been led astray by my loins. Loins and your pretty face."

"You have quite a way with words." He laughed, reaching for his boxers. "But you said I was pretty. Thanks for that."

"Aidan," I began, "I'm sorry. I think I'm deflecting with jokes and trying to push you away."

"You learned that from editing psychology textbooks, huh?"

"Maybe. This can't happen again."

"Okay." He grinned.

"I mean it."

"I hear ya, loud and clear."

"Why don't I believe that you believe me?"

"Wow."

"What?"

"People need espresso to keep up with you. Luckily, I comprehend Sibby without it."

"Aren't you talented…"

He grinned in a way that made me believe he was thinking of his other talents. Talents I would not be sampling again. It would be a bad idea.

Wouldn't it?

And then Aidan pulled me back down onto the bed of iniquity.

Who was I kidding? I wasn't a slave to my own loins—I was a slave to Aidan's.

"That was the last time," I panted the next morning, trying to recover my breath.

"Liar," Aidan said. "That last time was your idea."

"You complaining?"

"Do you hear me complaining? Also, do I get coffee before you kick me out this time?"

"You make me sound so heartless. You can have coffee and maybe even a muffin."

"Muffin? Is that a euphemism for something?"

"Shut up. I baked yesterday. Have a muffin and some coffee and we'll talk about stuff. Get it all ironed out before I see Annie for lunch. Oh, crap!"

"What now?"

"I've seen you naked! When we're at work, how am I supposed to pretend we haven't done the horizontal hora?"

"No idea. Good luck with that."

"No flirting at work. No leaving together, no showing up together, no drinking after work together."

"You said *together* a lot."

I rolled my eyes. "I'm just saying, there's a good chance we're gonna hook up again because, apparently, my loins have no willpower."

He laughed. "I really like your loins and their lack of willpower."

"Anyway. If we do something stupid again, which I think we inevitably will, then it can only happen here, in the confines of this apartment."

"I accept those stipulations."

"No dates."

"But—"

"No, Aidan. New York is small. Someone we work with will see us. And dating implies we're in a relationship. No relationship."

"I want two muffins," he muttered.

"Only if you eat them on the go."

"It's true what they say," Aidan said. "Crazy girls are the best in bed."

"Get. Out."

"He's the best dirty sex I've ever had," Annie admitted.

"Ew, ew, ew!" I said as I set down my burger and stopped chewing, a small piece of bread falling to the table from my mouth. "I don't need details."

"I wasn't giving you details," Annie said, "I was just glossing over everything by telling you he's the best—"

"Dirty sex you've ever had. Got it."

"How was Aidan?"

"Remarkable stamina. Acrobatic. That sort of thing."

She laughed. "You ever think we're kind of like *Sex and the City?*"

"We tried to be all *Sex and the City* in college, even going as far as using your two suite-mates as fillers."

"They weren't very good fillers," Annie said.

"I can't be a *Sex and the City* character. I'm fashion-challenged."

"You're right, you're a hipster."

"Watch it," I said. "Okay, confession time…" She nodded and I went on, "Aidan and I might have been in cahoots to get you and Caleb in the same place. Caleb apparently was very smitten with you. Or at least smitten with the dirtiness of you." I waited for Annie to blow up at me. Caleb was the first repeat guy in years, and that alone said something.

"I know," she said.

"What do you mean you know?" I demanded.

"Caleb already told me."

"Full disclosure? Sounds like boyfriend material to me."

"And Aidan? Is he boyfriend material?"

I stared at her for a long moment. "You going to eat all those fries?"

I answered the door and immediately jumped into Aidan's arms. He caught me with ease. "You smell like a restaurant," I said. I pecked his lips in rapid succession.

"It's an aphrodisiac," he said against my mouth. "I can lose it, if you let me use your shower."

"Yes. I just changed my sheets. I don't want that fried shrimp oil smell to linger. I'll get you a towel."

"You're going to have to disentangle yourself from me if you want me to shower."

"In a minute," I mumbled.

He walked out of the doorway and into the apartment, managing to shut the door. I reluctantly released my grip on him. "You look tired," I observed as I headed to the linen closet and pulled out a clean towel.

"It's one in the morning. And be glad you weren't working tonight. It was hell."

"What happened?"

"The computer system crashed. We couldn't print checks or process credit cards. No one carries cash anymore so people were stuck at the restaurant until we got the system online. They were pissed."

"Oh, man."

"Yep. And the kitchen lost three orders. Pure pandemonium."

"Yikes."

"You can say that again."

"Take a shower," I said. "I have some left over Thai food I can heat up for you."

Aidan grinned. "Chicken Massaman curry?"

"Maybe."

"That's my favorite. But I know it's not your favorite. You ordered it just for me, didn't you?"

I rolled my eyes. "Go shower."

After he showered, we settled onto the couch. Aidan wore nothing but boxers since it was the only piece of clothing that didn't smell. "I like your apartment," he said, pushing the finished plate of food away from him. "What's with the weird paint splattered wall?"

"I needed a change after Matt, but I got tired and gave up after one wall."

Aidan smiled and shook his head. "You're a ridiculous person."

"Glad you think so."

"Did you find this place with Matt?"

"No. I've lived here since I moved to the city. I'm subletting from a friend of the family. It's rent controlled. Only way I could afford it on my own. Of all the crappy things that happened recently, I'm just glad I didn't have to find a new apartment."

"Moving in this city sucks. It's so hard."

"I know." I scooted closer to him. "You tired?"

"A little."

"You full?"

"Sort of."

"You want to dirty some clean sheets?"

"Absolutely."

Chapter 10

Arancini [ah-rahn-chee-nee]:
    1. Fried risotto balls. Small, tapas size.
    2. Ha. Balls.

"Hello, Sibby," Katrina greeted in a thick Russian accent as she clocked in. She sounded more like Boris than Natasha, and I knew it was cliché, but it was true.

I stared at her for a full fifteen seconds before I replied. "Hello. You're talking to me."

"Yes."

"Why?"

"You've lasted two months. I can speak to you now."

"Two? Everyone told me it was three."

I swore her eyes twinkled with humor, but she didn't smile. "You have proven yourself."

"Thanks, I think."

She continued to stare at me with shrewd blue eyes.

"You need something," I said in sudden realization.

"I have date next Wednesday. Can you work for me?"

My calendar was wide open, what with having no real aspirations at the moment. "Sure."

"Really?"

"Of course."

She smiled. It transformed her face—it made her look almost...warm. She reached into her apron pocket, pulled out a candy bar, and snapped a square of chocolate loose in its foil. "You like chocolate?"

I took a square. "Thank you."

It felt like the equivalent of spitting on our palms and shaking hands.

Friend for life.

Jess entered the dining room and logged into the computer. She fiddled with buttons and counts of dishes, glancing at me out of the corner of her eye. "Did you iron your shirt?" she asked.

"Yes," I answered.

She fixed my cockeyed collar. "Then what's with all the wrinkles?"

"I swear I ironed it," I said, "but I had to put it in my bag to bring it."

"Okay. I guess I'll redraw the floor plan and put you inside where it's darker."

"You know," I said, "if you guys sprung for an iron, we'd be able to be wrinkle-free all the time."

"Logic, Sibby, what did we say about logic?" Zeb piped up.

"It has no place at Antonio's," I recited.

"Julian wants you guys to push oysters tonight," Jess said.

"You give me cookie, I sell oysters," Katrina stated.

Three hours later, it was the rush and my entire section was full. "Why do they do that?" I asked Zeb when there was a brief moment to catch my breath.

"Do what?" he asked.

"Seat my entire section when they could have easily rotated the sections. Like, you're half empty, but I'm totally full. Why?"

"Because that's the Antonio's way."

"Another one of those things I shouldn't ask questions about?"

"Yep."

"Excuse me, miss!" a woman in my section called.

I went over to a table with two women who had just gotten their entrées. "Hi, do you need something?"

"My steak is raw."

"I'm sorry, I thought you ordered it rare," I explained slowly.

"Yeah, but it's *raw*."

"You ordered it rare," I repeated. She blinked at me like *I* was the moronic one. I took a deep breath. "Would you like me to cook it more for you?"

She smiled. "That would be wonderful, thank you."

"How much pink?"

"Oh, uhm, just a little pink left."

I picked up the plate and headed back to the kitchen. I was terrified of Julian's reaction. I avoided the kitchen at all cost on the nights that he worked. Why couldn't it be the sous chef running the line?

"What's wrong with it?" Julian demanded. "That is a beautiful steak. A perfect steak!"

"She wants this cooked more."

He frowned in confusion. "She ordered it rare, no?"

"I don't want to talk about it."

"Oh my God! Sibby? Sibby Goldstein, *is that you?*"

I didn't immediately recognize the voice. When I looked at the owner of it, I realized it was one of the bitchy, mean girls from my high school days.

"Blakely!" I chirped with fake enthusiasm. "What are you doing here?"

"Eating," she tinkled with a laugh, tossing her long, thick, blond hair over a shoulder. The dim light caught the winking diamonds at her ears and on her finger. Princess cut. Large. Figured. "Do you work here?"

Blakely. Not the brightest bulb. "Yep."

"So random. Life's funny isn't it?" She ran a hand down her belly. Her slightly rounded, pregnant belly.

"I didn't know you lived in New York," I said.

"Yep. Went to college at NYU, where I met my husband. He's a very successful lawyer," she bragged. "I had no idea you lived in New York! I would've looked you up and we could've gone out for soy lattes and caught up."

"Yeah," I grimaced before forcing a grin. "That would've been swell."

"So you work here."

"So you're pregnant." I hoped Blakely wanted to keep talking about herself.

I was right.

She smiled like a woman who had never had any real problems. "My second," she explained. "The first is three. Are you married? Do you have kids?"

I looked at my wrist despite the fact that I didn't wear a watch. "Gosh, will you look at the time? I gotta get these drinks to the table. Good seeing you," I lied.

Blakely rummaged around in her Coach purse, pulled out a business card, and stuck it in my apron pocket. "Call me, I'd love to catch up." With a wave, she glided out of Antonio's, leaving me with a tray of drinks and a complete lack of self-worth.

I was dejected the rest of the night. I smiled and faked enthusiasm, but when I wasn't performing for customers, my mind was completely occupied with thoughts of Blakely and my direction in life. Or lack thereof.

It wasn't that I wanted what Blakely had—a husband and kids and a house in Long Island, but I wanted to figure out my dream.

I didn't have a dream.

What I did have: a chef yelling at me to sell oysters, a sexy manager who I was trying not to drool on, at least at work, and what was rapidly turning into a potential drinking problem. My head wasn't screwed on straight, not at all.

"You okay?" Nat asked at the end of the night. "Even your ponytail looks sad."

"I ran into a mean girl from high school."

"Ah, let me guess. She made you feel bad about where you are in life?"

I nodded. "Why is it life seems to work out so easily for nasty people? There's no justice in the world. She was head cheerleader, prom queen, and all that jazz. She was awful back then. Now she's married to a successful lawyer and wears a huge diamond on her finger. She has kids. She has what she wants."

"So she says," Nat said with a shrug. "She says she's happy, but you don't know. Maybe her husband is sleeping with his paralegal. Maybe her parents are getting a divorce. Maybe all the stuff she doesn't show people is really what keeps her up at night."

"Damn."

"What?"

"You're really good at this."

She grinned. "You have to stop looking at your life and wondering why it doesn't look like anyone else's. I'm a graphic artist, trying to break my way into illustrating children's books. It took me a long time to be okay with the starving artist thing."

"Thanks, Nat."

"Go home, get some sleep. In the words of Scarlett O'Hara, *Tomorrow is another day*."

"Are you hydrated," Zeb asked the next night.

"Yes," I said.

"Have you eaten?"

"Zeb, I'm not running in the marathon."

"You may as well be. You're working in an Italian restaurant the night before the New York Marathon. You have no idea what we're dealing with. No one will order appetizers or drinks, just pasta. Four hundred people. It's going to be bad. Very bad. Prepare for Armageddon. Prepare for Julian losing many tickets, breaking plates, and cursing in a mixture of French and English."

"Why do you work here?" I demanded.

"You still ask that question? Have you learned nothing?"

Seven hours later, I sat in between Zeb and Natalie in our usual after-work hangout, Johnny's. They were reliving the night while I sipped on bourbon. Zeb had attempted to warn me, but nothing came close to the experience.

"Sibby?" Natalie asked. "You okay?"

"Shell-shocked," Zeb surmised.

"Totally," Nat agreed.

"Well, it's good prep for the holiday season. The insanity gets even worse," Zeb said. "Large parties, people's already high expectations are even higher, and I get even bitchier."

"What!" I yelled. "I can't handle that. I could barely even handle tonight."

"You did fine," Nat soothed. "Better than fine. You handled it like a champ!"

My left eye spasmed. "You told me everyone was going to order pasta all night, but this was my night, ready: Do you have frozen margaritas? Do you have pizza? Do you have eggplant Parmesan, veal scaloppini, or any other clichéd Italian dishes? Can I get one hot pepper to see how hot it is before ordering them? What's *Al Dente*? Are you in college? How long have you worked here? Can you tell me every item in your chopped salad, even though I'm going to order the roast kale salad? These seats are too hard, do you have seat cushions? It's hot, can you turn down the heat? It's cold, can you turn on the heat? I'm a vegan, but I want to eat something that isn't a salad. Why is my dish bland? Is your salmon farm raised? Can I have my tiramisu decaf? Why have you stopped answering my questions? Why are you twitching? Why are you walking away? Miss? Miss!"

I fell silent. My co-workers stared at me for a long moment before they burst out laughing. I didn't think I was being funny, just honest. I dropped my head onto the table and let it rest there.

"I just want to go home."

"Drink some more bourbon," Natalie suggested.

"Okay," I said, lifting my head and taking an obligatory sip of my drink.

"Aidan seems different, doesn't he?" Natalie asked.

I snorted my drink and started coughing. Oh, the bourbon burn. Gah!

"Yeah, he was acting weird." Zeb looked at me.

"Really? I didn't notice anything different about him," I said. I was lying. I noticed everything about Aidan. I noticed his blue button-down shirt, every smile he threw at a customer, and how I had to actively not drag him into the wine room and have my way with him.

"He hasn't been himself all week. He didn't flirt with me at all," Natalie said. "Think he has a girlfriend?"

That was my cue to leave. "I gotta go home. I'm exhausted," I said, standing up. I threw a few bills down. "See you guys later."

"You're turning me into a night owl," I complained, though it wasn't really a complaint.

"Me? You're the one who won't leave me alone," he teased, wrapping an arm around my naked body.

I closed my eyes, drifting in and out of consciousness. "Should you go home?"

"You're going to make me do the walk of shame at 3:00 a.m.?"

I laughed and snuggled deeper into the bed. "If only you weren't such a good spooner, I'd be able to kick you out of my apartment. I think I need a list to remember this is casual. Number one, always kick you out, no matter what. Number two, no compliments. Not your size, eyes, or spooning abilities. Number three, don't feed the animals."

"You hungry? Let's order a pizza." Aidan climbed out of my bed and threw on his T-shirt and boxers.

"That violates rule number three."

"I'm not good at following rules." Aidan winked. I was glad he couldn't follow the rules. He was fun to have around, even when we weren't doing the dirty stuff. We laughed constantly. Every night that week, no matter if we worked together or not, he had come over to hang out. He always texted first, asking permission, and I always buzzed him up.

It was a very secret affair.

"So, what sort of perks do I get for sleeping with the manager?" I asked him when we were digging into the hot pepperoni pie. I'd grabbed us a few paper towels and two beers, and we sat on the living room floor and ate.

"You want a better schedule?" Aidan asked.

"Really?"

"No."

"Damn."

"You're new, you get the crappy schedule."

"It's not that crappy," I said. "What about wine at cost?"

"No."

"Why not? You guys get it in bulk and stuff!"

"Sorry, can't do it. Inventory, ya know? Can't hook you up."

"So sleeping with the manager gets me absolutely nothing, huh?"

"Hey, I bought you a pizza."

I grinned. "That's something."

"It would get you dates at cool restaurants and stuff, but you refuse to be seen in public with me. I think you're ashamed of me."

I rolled my eyes. "Have you seen you? Restaurant manager my ass. More like scruffy GQ model. And you actually have a great personality. Most hot guys are just abs

and nothing else. Oops, I broke rule number two
—compliments."

"You already broke rules two and three. You might as
well break rule number one. Can I stay the night?"

Chapter 11

Barolo [bah-RO-lo]:

1. Wine produced in the northern Italian region of Piedmont. Considered one of Italy's greatest wines.

2. Prestigious, expensive, and worth it.

"Watch my section," Katrina commanded.

"Only if you ask nicely," I said to her.

"That was me asking nicely."

"All right then," I said.

"You're lucky you're cute and small. I could crush you with my bare hands."

Bear hands, indeed.

"I respect the fear you instill in me," I said. "You ever see the old Bullwinkle cartoons?"

She frowned. "No. What is this?"

"Never mind. It's better that you don't know."

"I be back in five minutes."

Katrina disappeared into the bathroom and I walked through her section. Her table of four had shoved their menus aside and were talking with hand gestures. "Y'all ready to order?"

One man looked at me. "You're a lot shorter than our other waitress."

I smiled. "Good of you to notice. I'm also a lot less Russian."

"Excuse me!" the woman called out to get my attention. "EXCUSE ME!"

I shot an apologetic look at the really nice couple whose order I was trying to take and said, "I'm sorry, can you—"

"Absolutely," the middle-aged man said. His wife smiled at me in understanding.

Gosh, some people were really nice. I'd almost forgotten that.

I turned to the squawking woman behind me. "Yes?"

"I found a hair," she exclaimed dramatically.

I glanced at her plate. Three quarters of the dish had

been eaten, but I saw it. There. On the fork. A curly blond hair that perfectly matched the curly blond hair on the woman's head.

All the line cooks had dark hair.

I inwardly sighed, slapped an apologetic smile on my face and said, "Let me take that out of your way. Can I bring you something else?"

She shook her head. "No. I want a free drink. We all want free drinks." There were three other occupants at the table. They all stared at me with wide, not so innocent eyes. They were all brunettes, by the way.

My smile turned into a grimace as I took the dish with a strategically placed hair on it back to the kitchen. I flagged down Aidan.

"She found a blond hair in her food," I explained. "Should I also mention she's the only blond at the table?"

Aidan sighed. It was a weary sigh. Very Steinback. Sometimes this job got into your soul and sucked away at you until there was nothing left.

Okay. That was a bit dramatic. What could I say? I *had* been a theater major.

"Will you go deal with her? Please?"

"All right, but if I do, you so owe me."

"Do not, this is your job."

"Oh, right." He winked and left the kitchen. I stood by, watching him deal with the predators.

"This is ridiculous!" the unhappy woman hissed. "The customer is always right! What don't you understand about that?"

"Ma'am," Aidan began. "I am not allowed to give you free drinks. I can bring you another of what you ordered, or you can look at the menu and choose something else."

"Will I still have to pay for it?" she snapped, crossing her arms over her chest.

Aidan brought his fingers to his third eye and began to rub his head, the classic sign of a migraine. "Here's what I can do," he said finally. "I'll comp the entrée with the blond hair. And you and your friends can pay the check and leave."

"But—"

"Thank you for dining with us this evening." He stalked away.

I didn't get a tip, but I gave Aidan a high five.

"Come out with me and Caleb tonight," Annie said over the phone.

"I can't," I said. It was 4:00 p.m. on my day off, but I was still in pajamas, the rom-com on the TV paused.

"Why? Because Caleb is Aidan's friend and you have rules about hanging out with Aidan in public?"

"Aidan won't be there, he has to work," I said reflexively.

"Ah, your knowledge says it all."

"What does it say except that we work together?"

"Dude, you remember his schedule. So why won't you come out with me and Caleb?" Annie asked.

"Because I have a UTI."

Pause.

"No."

"Yes."

SAMANTHA GARMAN

"That sucks."

"Yep."

"I mean, really sucks."

"Being a woman sucks sometimes. I mean, come on, the lady problems we have to put up with? And seriously, I can't have some great sex without being cursed for it?"

"Apparently, you've been having a lot of great sex."

"And now I'm being punished," I sighed.

"I've been thinking about your situation," Annie began.

"Clarify, because I have a lot of situations."

"That you do. It was a blanket reference to all your situations. And your terrible luck. We should have a cleansing ritual of some sort."

"I cleaned the apartment, I splattered a wall, and I burned Matt's shirt. The one that had been overlooked since it was under the bed."

"Wait, you burned his shirt?"

"No, I didn't burn his shirt. Where would I burn his shirt?"

"I don't know, the fire escape?"

"Good point. What kind of cleansing ritual?"

"Burn some sage and tell the bad juju to go away."

"So, in other words, just drink. A lot."

"Pretty much."

I laughed. "I'm not supposed to drink while on antibiotics."

"Go back to watching your rom-com."

"I'm not watching a rom-com," I denied.

"Yeah, right. I know you."

After I finished the movie, I made myself a sandwich and then fell asleep on the couch. I woke up to a buzzing phone. It was Aidan, wanting to come over. I really just wanted to sleep in my bed by myself, spread out and get better. Besides, my hair was greasy and I looked like crap. I was never going to let Aidan see me when I looked like crap.

"Hey," he said.

"Hey."

"You were asleep, weren't you?"

"Yeah."

"Sorry. I'm done at work, can I come over?"

"I'm not feeling so hot," I evaded.

"What's wrong?"

"Oh, just a bug," I said. I was *so* not going to tell him about my UTI.

Not sexy.

"What kind of bug? Stomach bug?"

"Yes," I said. "I don't want to get you sick. And I'd rather just have my bed to myself."

"I get it. Feel better."

I hung up, wondering why I suddenly felt worse. I almost changed my mind and texted him to come over, but didn't. Boyfriends took care of their sick girlfriends. Hot hook ups did not take care of their...booty calls.

Booty call. I hated that term.

I brushed my teeth and washed my face, going through my minimal bedtime ritual. I was pulling back the covers of my bed when my phone rang.

"Hello?" I said.

"It's me," Aidan replied. "I know you said you're sick, so I brought you some soup and ginger ale."

"Oh," I said. "Thanks. I'll buzz you up." Shaking my head, I muttered, "Ah, crap."

Annie was over at my place after I'd recovered from my UTI, and we were catching up over homemade food and some wine. She had managed to pull herself away from Caleb and the Upper East Side. It was full-on girl talk time.

"Hold on," Annie said, gesturing at me with her fork. "You're telling me that even after you told him you were sick, he still came over?"

I nodded.

"With ginger ale and soup?"

I nodded again.

"Even when he thought you were puking your guts up?"

"We're eating here," I said as I pushed my plate of food away from me.

"Sorry. You do know you might have to marry this guy."

"You don't believe in marriage," I stated.

"But *you* do—and this guy—holy shit. He seems kind of amazing."

"The other shoe hasn't dropped," I said. "Let's wait a bit longer."

She shrugged. "I already like him better than Matt."

"Matt didn't set the bar real high by cheating on me. You finished?" I asked, picking up my plate and reaching for hers.

"What's for dessert?"

"Cupcakes," I said. "They're gluten free."

"You lie."

I grinned. "Totally. They'd suck if they were gluten free."

"Amen. I know you Brooklynites are all about your sugar free, gluten free, vegan friendly, cardboard tasting food, but come on! Butter keeps the hinges loose." She pretended to make a robot move with her arm, and then picked up a book, which was resting on the kitchen table. "Okay. I've been silent about this for an hour, but now it's time for you to explain."

"You know I like to read romance novels."

"Yes. But Fabio is on the cover of this one. He has giant man nipples. *Mipples*, if you will."

"It's a time travel romance," I answered. "Pretty good actually. The Salvation Army was having a book sale. I filled a box for five dollars."

"Let me guess, all of them are romance novels?"

I nodded. "I highlighted all the genitalia euphemisms."

"Why?"

"Because it's fun."

"You should write one of these," she said, tossing the book. It landed on the table with a soft thud.

"Excuse me?"

"You should. You read more than anyone I know. You devour these things. Why not give it a shot?"

"Annie," I said quietly. "I wrote plays in college. I don't know the first thing about writing a full-length novel."

She shrugged. "So what? What else are you doing?"

I glared at her.

"I mean, what do you have to lose?"

"These are festive," I said, holding up a weirdly shaped yellow gourd.

"Autumn is here," Zeb announced. "Did you see the ginormous pumpkin by the hostess stand? For the Thanksgiving staff meal, Julian will turn that pumpkin into pie."

"Yum."

"Come December, the restaurant will have wreathes, mini lights, and red bows everywhere."

"I can't believe I've been here four months already."

"Yeah, that's the danger of the restaurant world. You blink and five years goes by."

"Yikes." I glanced at the floor plan. "Oh, man. I'm in section one."

Section one was right by the bar where guests congregated before being seated. It was difficult to see my tables, much less actually get to them, and whenever I was in section one, I seemed to develop a twitch. Section one was what we called "no man's land". It was the section of sixty-dollar checks; people who came to a popular restaurant late on Saturday night without a reservation, expecting a table right away. Bussers hardly ventured into no man's land, and I was usually on my own.

"It's Saturday," Zeb said. "At least we'll be busy and the pain will be over fast."

"That was a lie."

"Yeah."

"I had another server nightmare the other day."

"Ah, you really are one of us now."

"I dreamed I had this entire dining room to myself, and I kept getting large parties, and I didn't understand the computer system to put in their orders. And even though technically, the kitchen was supposed to be closed, Jess kept seating me."

"I'm going to have a nightmare about your nightmare."

"I'm just glad I didn't dream about Julian."

"Oh, you will, believe me."

"Let's set up," I said. "The sooner this is over the better."

By eight o'clock, I was elbowing my way through the bar crowd, annoyed that no one heard my many pleas for them to move out of my way. I finally reached a couple that was ready to order.

"Any questions?"

"Do you have Wi-Fi?" the woman asked.

"No. Do you have any questions…about the menu," I clarified.

"Do you have kosher wine?" the man asked.

"Uh, we're an Italian restaurant, and our favorite ingredients come from a pig."

"Okay, then water's fine. My wife will have the truffle ricotta ravioli."

"I'm not that much of a ricotta fan," the woman interjected, failing to look up from her phone. "Is the ricotta really overwhelming?"

"Yeah, it's the main event."

"Oh, then you order, honey, and let me look at the menu again."

"I'll have the fettuccine with mushrooms," the man said, handing me his menu.

"And I'll have this pasta here." She pointed to the agnolotti filled with butternut squash. "What kind of noodle is it?"

"Basically a ravioli. Do you guys want to split a salad? The kitchen is busy and food is fresh to order, so you might wait a bit for your dinner."

"Do we get bread?" the man asked.

"Yes."

"Then we'll be okay." He reached for his water and took a sip.

"Can I get a straw for my water?" the woman asked.

"Sure."

I brought her a straw from the bar and then she asked, "Can I get lemons?"

"Of course. Is there anything else I can get you while I'm at the bar?"

"No, that'll do it."

I dropped off the plate of lemons and as I turned to leave, Mrs. Annoying grabbed my arm and asked for paper napkins and more bread. Twenty minutes later, after running around like a maniac, the Annoyings flagged me down yet again. I hoped it wasn't to change their order.

"Yes?" I asked, feeling a bit harassed.

"We're just wondering where our food is," Mr. Annoying said.

I blinked. "It's cooking."

"But it's pasta," Mrs. Annoying whined. "How long does pasta take to cook?"

I looked around the dining room, and when I turned back to them, my smile was more sugary than the crème brûlée on our dessert menu. "It's a Saturday night. Prime time. Would you like me to bring you that salad?"

She stared at me in confusion, like I was speaking Elvish. I took a deep breath and tried again, "I'll check with the kitchen." Even though I knew the answer. The Annoyings were going to wait. They would have had to wait even if they'd ordered an appetizer. This is what happened when you went to a restaurant that didn't use prepackaged food and microwaves.

I returned to my section. I had been gone, two, maybe three minutes, and that was all it took for everything to go up in flames. I had three newly seated tables waiting to be greeted, two tables needing to be cleared, and one ready to order dessert and coffee.

No man's land, indeed.

But before all that, I had to tell the Annoyings that they were going to have to wait another fifteen minutes for their food. Fifteen minutes at least.

Ugh.

Sometimes, people sucked.

"Sibby?"

"Hmmm?"

"Why are you standing in the corner with your head against the wall? Did Jess put you in timeout?" Zeb asked.

"No," I murmured. I was near the hostess stand, off the main floor. I just needed a minute to get it together.

"I don't speak Crazy. Translate for me."

"My tables. They're terrible."

He sighed. "They broke your spirit, didn't they?"

135

"Yes."

"What did they do?"

"You want the highlights?" I asked, finally lifting my head from the brick wall and turning towards him.

He grimaced. "You have an indentation on your face." He pointed to his own forehead. "Right in the center."

"Lovely."

"So, your tables…"

"Right. I had a table tip in coins."

"Ouch..."

"Yeah. Maybe I shouldn't have laughed directly at them when they asked if we had smoothies."

"Maybe you shouldn't have," he agreed.

Nat opened the door in between the main dining room and the walkway to the host stand. She held out a black check presenter.

"What's this?"

"Credit card slip from your six top."

"I can't look at it," I stated. "I can't take any more."

Nat grinned. "You might want to look at it."

Doing as bid, I flipped it open and glanced at the tip line. An extra sixty dollars on top of twenty percent. "Holy shit!" I showed it to Zeb.

"Damn! Is your faith in humanity restored?"

"For the time being."

Chapter 12

Nocello [no-chell-oh]:

    1. A liqueur made from green walnuts.

    2. Liquid sex.

"Do you ladies want dessert tonight?" I asked.

"Nah, we're just going to drink our calories," one woman said.

"And emotions," the other added.

"I respect that." I took the dessert menus away, smiling as I went. They seemed really familiar—maybe because they reminded me of my best friend and me.

Good times.

"What's that smell?" Zeb asked as he strolled by me, carrying a tray of clean wine glasses. He set the tray on the bar and began unloading them.

"Ah, that would be me," I said. "I spilled a tray of dirty martinis on myself."

"How?"

"This is me we're talking about."

Zeb laughed. "How is it your tip average is consistently over twenty percent?"

"Because with me, you don't just get dinner. You get dinner and a shit show. I'm entertainment—a full on comedy of errors."

"You are that," Zeb agreed.

"How much stock is back there?"

"Uh, seriously?"

"Yeah."

"You haven't seen it?"

"I haven't been able to get back there. I had a table demand my life story. They asked if I was still in college, and thinking it would be easier to lie, I just said yes. And then told them I was a creative writing major at NYU. That opened up a can of worms."

"You lied to a table?" he feigned shock.

"They don't get the truth," I said. "They get a smile and some food. That's it."

"Welcome to the dark side."

"Glad to be here."

"I was trying to be stock bitch, but it just kept coming. There's still about eight racks of glasses and two buckets of silverware."

I sighed. "Stock is my version of Sisyphus rolling the boulder up the mountain."

"Amen. Kirk and I are going out for a drink after work," Zeb said. "Wanna come?"

"Thanks, but after all this, I'll be ready to go home."

An hour later, I was walking to the subway. I sent a text to Aidan, asking if he wanted to come over after he finished closing the restaurant. I didn't get a reply right away, so I hopped on the train. Whenever I really wanted to get home, the train creepy-crawled from 1st Avenue to Bedford Avenue, turning a fifteen-minute journey into a forty-five minute one.

By the time I got above ground, I still didn't have a response from Aidan. I got home, showered off the dirty martinis, and crawled into bed. Still no response from Aidan, which was weird, but I made myself turn off my phone.

That lasted about five minutes.

My final shred of self-respect had gone the way of the Dodo as I fell asleep clutching my cell phone, waiting for a text from my non-boyfriend.

I woke up the next morning to a text message from Aidan. It had come in around 2:30 a.m. saying he was going to spend the next few nights at his place.

Aidan had not shown me an ounce of distance. Not since we'd taken our relationship from spooning to the dirty stuff. Now there was this. I'd never experienced such distance in the form of a text message.

Crap. I might've become a clinger.

Annie came over for Sunday brunch, and as I got the fixings for the French toast, she pulled out ingredients for Bloody Marys. I'd once spent a Thanksgiving with Annie's family when we were in college. They started their Thanksgiving with Bloody Marys in the morning. I didn't remember the rest of the day.

I sipped cautiously as I flipped a piece of bread, jazz playing in the background on my Bose speaker.

Annie said, "I have to tell you something."

"You're not engaged, are you?"

"What? God, no!"

"Pregnant?"

"Nope."

"Whew. I don't think I could take any more upheavals. Tell me what's up."

"I saw Aidan last night."

"Okay."

"He was out at one of my favorite bars. And I saw him with a girl. They were laughing and clearly having a good time."

The spiciness of the Bloody Mary began to surge back up into my throat. I choked down the horseradish, gripping my spatula, all the while trying to maintain my calm.

But calm and I didn't have a good relationship.

"We're casual," I said, striving to be rational. I paused a long while.

"Sibby—"

"What?"

"The French toast is burning."

"Shit!" Smoke began to fill the kitchen and after a moment the smoke alarm went off. Annie dashed to the window and propped it open. I turned off the stove and began to fan a dishtowel near the smoke alarm.

"Were you with Caleb?" I asked once the smoke alarm silenced.

"No. I was with a friend from culinary school."

"Did you ask Caleb about it?"

"No. Bros before hoes."

I breathed a sigh of relief. "Thanks." Against my better judgment, I downed the spicy Bloody Mary in a few gulps.

"Another?" Annie asked, already heading for the supplies.

"Keep them coming."

"You have blackberry jam on your face."

"Saving it for later," I muttered, reaching for a napkin. "Did I get it?"

She shook her head, took my napkin, and dabbed at my mouth.

"God, I really can't do day drinking anymore." I sat up, putting a hand to my head. "All men are couch canoes."

"I think you mean douche canoes. And not all of them suck," Annie said.

"Yeah, I don't believe that. First, I get Matt, who was so far in the closet he was finding Christmas presents, and now I get Aidan with his cheating. I'd never cheat on a guy!"

"He's not technically cheating..."

"It feels like cheating." I buried my head in my hands.

"Maybe he's not with her…"

"What other explanation is there?" I asked.

"Okay, I'll admit between our track records, we jump to conclusions."

"The other night I asked if he wanted to come over after work and he said he'd be sleeping at his place for a few days."

"I'll text Caleb."

"No, don't. I'm not going to be that girl."

"What girl is that?"

"The insecure girl who wants to know what her casual hook-up is doing. God, I'm so stupid. I should be the girl who focuses on her career. But I don't have one of those."

"I still think you should write a romance novel."

"I'm gonna try," I vowed.

"Really?"

I nodded and then slumped over in my chair, my head resting on the kitchen table.

"I think we should start drinking water," Annie said, getting up.

"Yes. And you know what? I'm going on a cleanse."

"Does that mean we have to stop drinking?"

"Not that kind of cleanse. I mean a life and man cleanse. I need to get rid of everything that sucks. If I have any chance of getting my self-worth back, I need to focus on me and not guys. Especially not guys who have super-hero moves in bed." I got up and wobbled my way to the living room, collapsing onto the couch.

"Superhero?" Annie asked from the kitchen. I heard her filling a glass of water and she came back, plopping down on the floor. She took a drink and then handed it to me.

"Thanks. Yeah, superhero. Aidan deserves a cape."

God, he'd look good in a cape. And spandex.

No! The guy was slime!

"How the hell am I supposed to work with him? Gah! I knew I shouldn't have slept where I ate!"

"I think you meant shit where you eat," Annie corrected. "But yeah, the end result is the same."

I was an ostrich style head-in-the-sand sort of person. My relationship with Matt had been full of red flags by the time he'd cheated on me. I had also ignored the fact that my office job had been giving me fewer and fewer projects. Deep down, I knew I was a reactive person—not a proactive one.

But no more.

I was done being the girl things happened to. Aidan had gone silent commando for three days and been seen with another girl, and that only reminded me I needed to get my crap together.

Focus, focus, focus.

Usually, I wore stud earrings and next to no makeup to work. I would just have to shower it off later. But I wanted to give Aidan a good old *screw you*, so I wore dangly silver fork charm earrings, mascara, blush, and lipstick. And even though I'd have to change into my unflattering, boxy server uniform, I wore cute jeans that showed off my butt.

I put in my ear buds and played "Eye of the Tiger" on repeat while I rode the train to work. I could do this!

And then I walked into Antonio's.

Damn the guy. Aidan looked hot in dress pants and a button-down. The fact that I hadn't seen or heard from him for three days only made me want him more. Wanting what you couldn't have was so true. Only I'd had Aidan, and it wasn't enough. I wanted to devour him. All of him in his newly clean-shaven hotness.

"Hi," I chirped as I came in through the front door.

He looked at me curiously. "Hi. You're in a good mood. You okay?"

"What, I'm not allowed to be in a good mood when I come to work?"

"I guess…just…you sure you're okay? You look a little flushed."

"I'm peachy!"

I sauntered downstairs, making sure to put an extra jaunt in my step. I changed into work clothes and then made my way back upstairs and settled in for the pre-setup staff meeting. I smiled to myself when I saw Aidan couldn't take his eyes off me.

It would be a long night—for him.

"I want a red wine with little to no tannins. What do you suggest?" the woman asked.

"Pinot Grigio," I said flatly.

Her date snorted into his glass of water and then set it

down to reach for his napkin. The woman didn't find me funny.

"I'll bring you a taste of something and you can tell me if you like it."

After the woman was happily enjoying the Grenache I'd suggested, Aidan came up to me and asked, "Hey, do you have a second?"

"Yeah."

"I want to talk to you about the schedule," he stated, though his eyes said that was a cover for what he really wanted to discuss.

I told Zeb to watch my section and then I followed Aidan downstairs. We went into the office and he closed the door to give us privacy. I raised an eyebrow. "Won't people wonder what we're doing down here with a closed office door?"

He shrugged. "So we'll tell them you had a problem with a co-worker."

"But I don't have a problem with any of my co-workers. I get along with everyone. Even Katrina."

"What about me?" he demanded. "You have a problem—with me."

"What are you talking about?"

"You're not acting like yourself."

"And that would be…"

"You're wearing makeup," he pointed out. "And you straightened your hair. And you wore really tight jeans. Like, second-skin tight. I've hung out with you enough to know you hate second skin clothes."

"Aidan, can you please get to the point? I have a full section upstairs."

"Annie saw me with another girl. She got drunk and told Caleb."

"Aidan, don't—"

"The girl is my sister."

"I just—wait what?"

"Sister. She lives in California. She flies out randomly to visit me. The reason I didn't come to your apartment after work the other night was because she was waiting for me."

I smacked his upper arm. "You couldn't tell me that? You had to let me wonder for three days why I didn't see you?"

"But don't people only explain themselves to each other when they're in a relationship? Did I really owe you an explanation?"

I sighed. "I see your point."

"And what about you? You couldn't just come out and ask me about the other girl?"

"So, she's really your sister? You weren't drinking, cavorting, and hooking up with buxom blondes?"

"I'm not into blondes."

"No?"

"I'm into walking disaster brunettes."

I didn't smile at his teasing tone. I took a deep breath and said, "You ever want out, you tell me."

"I don't want out."

"Not right now you don't. Just, in the future. I can't handle another Matt situation."

"Okay," he said with a nod. "Same goes for you."

"Okay," I agreed.

"I'm sorry, Sibby. I didn't mean to make you—doubt me. I should have realized after Matt that you would—well, anyway. I'm sorry."

"Thank you," I said sincerely.

"We good?"

"We're good."

"So tonight? After work, can I come over?"

I grinned and shrugged. "Maybe."

"Tease."

I laughed. "I'll see you after work." I got up, needing to head back to the floor and my tables. I ran up the stairs and opened the door to the dining room, then came to an abrupt halt. Aidan knocked into my back and I almost went flying.

"Oops, sorry. You okay?" he asked.

I didn't answer. My heart began to beat like I'd had too much caffeine. My eyes widened and my palms got gross and clammy.

No.

Matt was sitting across the table from the man he had cheated on me with. They were on a date, like in public, for real.

That was the thing about New York. Millions of people, and you always saw the one you didn't want to see.

"Sibby? What's wrong? You haven't moved."

I didn't reply as I scurried towards the kitchen, wanting to hide, wanting to be able to pretend I'd never seen him.

System overload.

As I approached the heavy wood door of the kitchen, a busser was on his way out with a full tray of glasses. I pushed in as he pushed out; he had more power and the door swung back—colliding with my nose. There was a solid snap of cartilage and a spray of blood.

I went down hard.

Man, I really hoped I didn't need plastic surgery.

Chapter 13

Sambuca [sam-boo-ka]:

    1. An Italian aniseed-flavored liqueur.

    2. Tastes like licorice. It's disgusting.

I was on the floor on my back, feeling like a rookie boxer who'd lost an important match.

"Sibby? Sibby can you hear me?" Aidan demanded.

"My nose…" I wheezed, tears streaming from my eyes.

Aidan cursed. The commotion around me barely penetrated my shocked senses. He scooped me off the floor and held me against his chest. Someone handed me a rag so I could stem the flow of blood.

"Don't let Matt see," I whispered, attempting to shield my face as Aidan carried me through the dining room.

"Matt?" Aidan asked. "Your ex?"

I pointed in Matt's general direction.

"I'll make sure he doesn't see you." Aidan called out for someone to get me a bag of ice. My nose throbbed in protest, but I kept the ice to my face, vaguely wondering how bad the swelling was going to be, and vowing that I wouldn't look in a mirror for at least a week.

"You're really lucky," Aidan said. "I don't think your nose needs surgery, but I'm taking you to the hospital to be safe."

"You don't have—"

"Yes, I do."

We got into a cab out in front of Antonio's, and Aidan held my hand on the drive to Beth Israel. We waited in silence for over an hour for the doctor to see me. Pretty fast considering it was New York City. The doctor on call checked out my face, told me not to blow my nose no matter what I did, and gave me a heavy-duty painkiller. He exchanged my melted bag of ice for an ice pack, and then handed me a prescription for high-end pain meds.

"You're lucky you don't need plastic surgery. Your nose is still straight and the skin didn't split. It's more of a fracture, really," he said. "Just ice it and take the pain killers sparingly. They will knock you out, so be careful to only take them as prescribed, okay?"

"Thanks," I muttered.

Aidan guided me outside and hailed a cab. The ride back to Brooklyn took about twenty minutes, and by then, the horse tranquilizer I'd popped at the hospital was having its way with me. We hit a twenty-four-hour pharmacy and got my prescription filled.

"Is my neck still attached to my head?" I asked Aidan when we were climbing the stairs to my apartment.

"You mean is your head still attached to your neck? Yes."

"My tongue feels fuzzy," I said.

"They gave you some heavy-duty pain meds and you're a lightweight." He took my keys from me and unlocked my door.

"Who's that character in Charlie Brown with the black cloud that follows him around wherever he goes?" I asked.

"I have no idea," Aidan said.

"This is just great," I muttered as Aidan maneuvered me onto the couch. "I had the perfect nose, you know? Small and dainty. No doctor's scalpel has ever touched it. Unheard of in the Goldstein family."

"Yes, your nose belongs on a Roman coin," Aidan agreed. Perhaps he was humoring me. I didn't care. I was too high and too miserable to care.

"This has to be it, right? How much more crap am I supposed to deal with? I mean, my life is a slapstick comedy. One of those plays where people come and go, slamming doors, and by the end, your stomach hurts from all the laughing?"

"I think you mean a farce."

"Farce, yes."

After Aidan set me on the couch, he headed to the kitchen, opened the freezer, pulled out a bag of frozen peas and brought it to me.

"No, thanks. I'm not hungry."

"It's for your nose."

"Oh, right. Do we have ice cream?"

"Yes."

I winced as I changed the ice pack while he retrieved the ice cream. He sat down next to me. "I'll feed it to you."

"You don't have to."

"I want to."

"Okay. I want you to."

"That's the drugs talking."

"Maybe. Why does Matt keep popping up like a whack-a-mole? Is this the universe's way of telling me to deal with crap? By shoving my gay ex-boyfriend in my face every five minutes?"

"Eat this." He spooned ice cream into my mouth.

It was awkward.

I felt like I could pass out where I sat in the soiled bloody restaurant clothes I still wore. "You're really nice. Except for the last three days. You were a butt. Staying away."

"Have you ever liked someone more than they liked you?"

"Uhm, pretty much every guy I've ever dated."

"I don't believe that." Aidan took a bite of ice cream.

"We're sharing the same spoon," I sighed.

High as a mother-effing kite.

"That okay?"

"Okay? It's perfect." My eyes started to close. "I need to Feng Shui my life."

I might've kept on muttering, but I had no idea since I fell into a deep, drugged, glorious sleep. When I awoke, it was sometime in the middle of the night and I was still on the couch, propped up. I was still breathing through my mouth and my nose throbbed.

Great. Creepy mouth-breather.

Aidan was asleep in the chair next to the couch. He'd discarded his button-down shirt and slacks, but he'd left his socks and boxers on. On the coffee table, I saw two of my prescription pills next to a full glass of water.

Aidan had set them out for me. The sweetheart.

"Awwww," I whispered, picking up the pills and swallowing them down with water. Wanting to see the damage to my face, I crept into the bathroom and flipped on the light.

To say it was bad was a drastic understatement. Not only was my nose swollen and red, but both of my eyes were black. I looked like Mexican skull art.

"Thought you weren't going to look in the mirror," Aidan said in a sleepy voice, standing in the doorway of the bathroom.

"Distract me, quickly, please, so I don't cry. If I cry it will hurt and I already can't breathe through my nose."

"At least your glasses didn't break," Aidan said.

"My life is so pathetic."

"Sibby, Sibby, wake up!" someone called.

"No," I muttered, my eyelids attempting to flutter open.

"Sibby!"

"Stop shaking me!" I finally opened my eyes and looked into the concerned face of Aidan. "Why are you looking at me that way?"

"You're having an allergic reaction," he stated.

"Huh?"

"To the pain pills you took last night. You were scratching your arms in your sleep."

I looked down at my body. Red bumps covered my arms and legs. "Oh, God. My face! Is it on my face?"

He nodded solemnly. I sprang up from the bed and rushed to the bathroom. I let out a wail when I looked in the mirror. My cheeks were red and splotchy. I started to itch.

"What do I do?" Aidan demanded. "Tell me what to do?"

"You can't panic. I'm already panicking. Too much panic!" I hobbled out of the bathroom and went to the coffee table. I grabbed my phone, and without thinking, I hit speed dial number two.

My father answered on the first ring. "Hello, my absent daughter," he said. "Where have you been?"

"Around," I said.

"That sounded slutty," Aidan whispered.

I glared at him. "Dad, what do I do if I took Vicodin and I'm now having an allergic reaction?"

"Why did you take Vicodin?" he demanded. "That's some heavy-duty stuff."

"I hurt myself," I evaded.

"Ankle? Wrist?"

"No—my nose. I broke my nose."

"How did—"

"Swinging door. I'll fill you in later. Right now, I need to stop the itching and the bumps."

"Benadryl should do the trick."

"Really?"

"Really. Let me know if it works—and I want the full story when you're up for it."

I sighed. "Okay. Love you, Dad."

"Love you, too."

I hung up with my father and went to the bathroom

153

again, opening the cabinet. I found Benadryl, read the label, and popped a few.

"Why did you call your Dad?" Aidan asked from the doorway of the bathroom.

"He's a doctor."

"You going to tell him the truth about stuff?"

"Some stuff."

He sighed, reached out, and stopped my hands from rubbing my arms. "You can't scratch. You'll scar."

"How do I stop?"

"You sure you're going to be okay?" Aidan asked, heading for the front door.

"Relatively," I said. "You have to go to work."

"I could call out."

"Then everyone would know."

He sighed.

"I'm just going to sit at home and maybe bake some-thing. It's all I can manage on Benadryl."

"Bad idea. Order food. You shouldn't be cooking. Seriously."

"Okay."

Aidan gently kissed me on the forehead and my heart melted like a stick of butter. "Call me if you need anything, okay? Promise?"

"Promise. Thanks, Aidan. For taking such good care of me."

He kissed me again and I waved my oven mitts at him. He'd taped my hands up so I couldn't scratch. I felt like a kid with chicken pox.

I waited until I knew he was gone before finding a way to pull off the oven mitts and ordering some food. And then I proceeded to sit on my hands so I wouldn't scratch. When the buzzer sounded, I hit the intercom button and said, "Yes?"

"Delivery for Sibby Goldstein."

I buzzed the deliveryman in, thinking it was my take-out. I waited to hear his footsteps on the stairs. The man's face was hidden due to the large bouquet of flowers he was carrying.

"You look like you're being attacked," I teased as I took them from him. "Thank you." I made it back inside before he could see the mess of my face.

I closed the door and took the large, fragrant, colorful bouquet to the coffee table, wondering who could possibly be sending me flowers. I managed to open the envelope by using my one free hand and my teeth and then read the note, "Get Well Soon!" Everyone from Antonio's, even Julian, the crazy French chef had signed it.

"Don't cry, don't cry, don't cry," I said, knowing I'd be stuffy for hours if I gave in. I wondered how the hell I was going to occupy myself for the next week or so until my nose was healed enough to work. Halloween had already come and gone so scaring customers was out of the question. Too bad. I could've gone as a zombie.

Maybe it was time to get serious about this romance novel writing idea. I had the time. I had a flexible job.

What was I waiting for?

It was day four of being locked up in my apartment, and I was going stir crazy. I thought about painting the rest of the walls just to have something to do—instead, I forced myself to sit down and outline a book idea.

After an hour of getting nowhere, I decided to try out a new fudge recipe. My phone buzzed with a text from Zeb. He and Natalie were on their way over to cheer me up.

"You look like hell," Zeb said as a way of greeting.

"If you're going to talk to me that way, I won't let you into my apartment."

"He doesn't mean it," Natalie said.

"Bullshit. She looks like a horror film extra." Zeb held up a bag. "Besides, I've got the wine so I can pretty much say whatever I want."

"You should've seen me a few days ago—I had an allergic reaction and the pain meds gave me hives."

"How...your life...man..." Nat said.

I waved them inside.

"It smells like Willy Wonka's Chocolate factory in here," Nat said in amazement. I closed the door and took a few of their bags and put them on the kitchen table.

"I made fudge," I explained.

"God, you get so much done," Zeb said.

"I'm housebound," I reminded them. "What else am I going to do?"

Once we were seated at the table, wine and food ready,

Nat finally asked, "Okay, so can you tell us what the hell happened?"

"I broke my nose," I said.

"Obviously." Zeb rolled his eyes.

"What did Aidan tell people?"

They exchanged a look. "Not much," Nat admitted.

"You are so lucky," Zeb groused.

"Uhm, really? How do you figure?" I demanded.

"You go to the hospital and Aidan goes with you? Hot."

"You're sick," Nat said.

"It wasn't like a date, you know. I saw my ex-boyfriend —out with a dude, by the way. Like, finally out-out." Two pairs of eyes blinked at me. "I didn't want Matt to see me, so I headed back to the kitchen. Rudolpho was coming out of the kitchen and I was going in. Cue swinging door. Next thing I know, I'm on the floor and Aidan is there with me."

Silence fell between us and Nat opened her mouth to speak but nothing came out. Zeb, on the other hand, had no such trouble with his filter. "Holy shit. You turned a guy gay?"

I glared at him. "You don't turn a guy gay. He was gay, he just…didn't know it."

"Until you," Zeb pointed out. "Show me a picture of him."

"Why? You think you can tell when I couldn't?"

He nodded. "Gaydar for gay boys is different than gaydar for girls."

I whipped out my cellphone and scrolled through my photos, showing him one of Matt and me standing at the top of the Empire State Building. "Oh, honey…"

"What?" I demanded. "How can you tell?"

He put two fingers to his head like antennae. "Beep… beep…beepbeepbeep!"

"You are *so* not good at this supportive friend thing," I said heatedly.

Zeb said, "You ever think about seeing a shrink? Might help you work through some stuff."

"I don't need a shrink. I need wine. Pass me the damn bottle."

"Catch me up on all the Antonio's gossip," I demanded when we were well into the bottle of wine.

"What did you miss, what did you miss," Zeb muttered. "Oh! The other night Julian yelled at Katrina because she didn't get a fifteen top's order in before the rush and then they had to wait forty-five minutes for entrees."

"Julian yelled at Katrina?" I asked in shock. "No."

"Yep," Nat agreed. "It was a sight to behold. She went all Mother Russia on him. Started throwing plates—at him."

"Cursing too. Damn, that chick can curse! I'm pretty certain she threatened him with her mafia connections."

"Antonio's is a regular melting pot, huh?" I shook my head. "I missed all that? Damn it!"

"The only way to calm her down was to offer her a tray full of cookies." Zeb smirked.

"Holy crap."

"Aaron came in wearing a new tracksuit. Purple velour.

Looked like a Soprano's extra," Nat said. "What else, what else?"

"I think that's it," Zeb said.

"No," Nat said. "That isn't it. Julian came into the restaurant happy yesterday. You didn't work so you didn't know."

"Julian? Happy?" Zeb shook his head. "Nope, don't buy it."

"He was whistling."

Zeb and I exchanged a glance. "He either got laid, or he got a dog," I said.

"That was pretty much my line of thought," Nat said.

"Maybe he got both!" Zeb suggested.

"Don't get carried away," I said. "This is still Julian."

"Yeah. The happiness won't last," Zeb said. "It never does."

Chapter 14

Fegato Alla Veneziana [FEH-gah-toh ah-lah Ven-eh-see-ahn-ah]:

    1. Calf's liver and onions.

    2. I don't do organs.

"Your fudge is amazing," Aidan said later that night long after Zeb and Nat had left. He reached for another piece.

"Thanks. So, have you noticed anything interesting about Julian the last few days?"

"Interesting? No."

"Nat claimed he was—happy."

"Happy?"

"Whistling when he came into work the other day."

"Julian. Whistling? She must've been hearing things."

I peered at him. "You know something."

"Nope."

"You do!"

"Can't tell you," he said. "Top Secret."

"You suck. You really can't tell me?" I muttered.

"I really can't. Seriously."

I sighed and changed the subject. "I washed a few of your T-shirts and stuck them in the top drawer of my dresser." I looked up at him. He was staring at me with a smug smile. "What?"

"You did my laundry?"

"I didn't do *your* laundry. I did *my* laundry and some of your clothes just happened to need washing. Seemed like a waste not to do them."

"And the drawer?" Aidan asked.

"What was I supposed to do? Dump your clean clothes on the floor?"

"Can I ask another question?"

I picked up a piece of fudge and stuffed it into Aidan's mouth. "Try." He mumbled some words around the fudge, but they were indecipherable. "I'll give you one hundred dollars to whistle right now."

Aidan's blue eyes twinkled as he chewed and swallowed. "You're really not going home for Thanksgiving?"

"How can I? I have to be back at the restaurant the next day."

"So what are you going to do for Thanksgiving if you're not going home?"

"I don't know. I was thinking of spending it with

Annie. She's gotta work this year. Her boss is throwing a Thanksgiving dinner for twenty-five. I'll probably pretend to help in the kitchen, but actually just sit and peel carrots while drinking." I was babbling. Sugar comas did that to me.

He looked at me. "You okay?"

"It's the sugar," I explained.

"I haven't gone home for Thanksgiving in a few years," Aidan said. "But this year, I have a few days off before the holiday and I was going to head home."

"Where is home?" I asked, realizing in all the time we'd been…spooning, I didn't know where he was from.

"Few hours Upstate."

"What's Thanksgiving like with your family?"

"My dad shoots the turkey himself if that gives you any idea." A bubble of laughter came out of my mouth and Aidan looked sheepish and adorable. "My mother's pecan pie is so sweet no one can eat more than a single piece. My two older sisters will be there with their husbands and kids. It's loud and always a full house. I always end up sleeping on an air mattress. But my youngest sister will stay in California. She's a free spirit. Doesn't believe in holidays."

"Jeez, sounds like a lot goes on."

"Yep." Aidan grinned. "Do you wanna come?"

I blinked. "Huh?"

"Great response."

"What are the holiday rules for naked friends?" I demanded.

"I have no idea. Do you want to come Upstate with me or not? And before you give me all these reasons why you can't—"

"I'd love to go home with you," I blurted out.

"Yeah?"

162

"Yes," I nodded. "Sugar makes me crazy, apparently. But, yes, Aidan, I'd love to spend Thanksgiving with you and your family."

It was two days before Thanksgiving and Grand Central Terminal was a zoo, even though it was only ten in the morning. Everyone was in a hurry, looking harassed and frazzled. Holidays did that to people, especially in New York. I stood by the clock, waiting for Aidan as he bought our tickets.

"You're insane," my best friend said over the phone.

"Yeah, I know."

"You're going to Aidan's home with a broken nose and two black eyes."

"My eyes are dark purple now," I interjected. "Besides, he already told his mom what happened. No one will be surprised."

"Wear concealer. That's all I'm saying."

"How's the turkey coming?" I asked, changing the subject.

"You mean the twenty-five pound frozen carcass I have defrosting in the sink? Great. Heather is driving me to drink."

"Flask?"

"Yep."

"Vodka?"

"Yeeeep."

"Happy defrosting!"

"Happy—whatever the hell it is you're doing. Call me when you're back in the city."

I saw Aidan as he wove his way through the herd of people. He adjusted his shoulder bag and took my wheeled suitcase before I could protest.

"Thanks," I said, hoisting up the bags full of wine. I wanted to make a good impression on his family—and thank them for having me. Six bottles of wine might have been overkill though.

"There's a good chance they'll kick me out of the family and adopt you instead."

"Have you ever brought a girl home for a holiday?" I asked when we were settled in our seats.

"I had a girlfriend freshman year in college. I brought her home. She didn't make it to the next Thanksgiving. My family scared her off."

"Then she wasn't worth it."

The train pulled away and Aidan looked at me.

"What?" I asked.

"You're not that much of a mess, are you?"

"Is that a compliment?"

"Just an observation."

"You don't seem to be a mess either. And that *is* a compliment."

His oldest sister waited for us at the train station. She was covered in flour and sugar and I thought I saw a piece of stuffing in her hair. Her smile was bright and she seemed to take my battered appearance in stride.

"Janet, Sibby. Sibby, Janet," Aidan said.

"Nice to meet you," I said. "Sorry about my face..."

"Oh, honey, please. I have three boys. I've seen worse," Janet said.

I relaxed immediately, and later I managed to hold on to my feelings of comfort when we entered Aidan's parents' house. As Aidan set down our bags, he was attacked by a monsoon of nieces and nephews.

"All right, you ruffians!" an older woman called, coming out of the kitchen, brandishing a wooden spoon. "Run out back and go play with the dogs."

I assumed she was Aidan's mother because he looked just like her. I saw where Aidan got his blue eyes and dark hair. His height must have come from his father, because Aidan's mother was pint-sized—smaller than me, which said something.

"Nice to meet you, Mrs.—" She cut me off with a hug.

"Call me Nancy." She pulled back to look at my face.

"It looks better than it did," I blurted out awkwardly.

"You sure?" she teased. "It looks pretty terrible."

"I got into a fight with a door—the door won."

"I'll say."

Aidan took me around the house, introducing me to his other sister, Melanie, and a bunch of kids whose names I'd never remember. "Where is your dad?"

"Hunting the turkey with the boys."

"You weren't kidding," I whispered to Aidan. To Nancy, I said, "Can I help with something?"

"Yes," she said. "Will you chop the pecans? Melanie!"

Melanie popped her head into the kitchen. "What's up?"

"Will you get Sibby something to drink?"

Melanie smiled, went to the stove, and ladled out something hot. I tasted apple and rum. It was delicious. Before I knew it, I was on my second one, laughing and talking with the women of Aidan's family, feeling accepted and welcomed.

"Your family can drink," I mumbled that night as Aidan and I got ready for bed. His mother insisted we take the sleeper sofa, and though I'd raised my eyebrows at our sleeping arrangement, Aidan seemed unfazed.

"We're good at it," he agreed.

"Your family is…"

"Insane?"

"Wonderful. Just the nicest people ever." Aidan's father,

Bud, had returned late in the afternoon holding two turkeys. He'd immediately cracked open a beer, looked at me, and while pretending he didn't see my black eyes and broken nose, gave me a bear hug for the record books. The brothers-in-law made jokes and treated me like another sibling. We went all of five minutes before they dubbed me "Bruiser".

"They like you."

"How can you tell?"

"You don't get a nickname unless they like you. And they teased you at dinner, didn't they? They wouldn't tease someone they didn't like."

We settled into the springy sofa mattress and pulled up the covers when I said, "I don't think I'll be able to sleep on my stomach ever again."

"Yeah, no one stands a chance when Mom is cooking."

"She kept filling my plate."

"She thinks you're too thin."

"Too thin? I had to unbutton my jeans at the dinner table."

"Sibby," he whispered.

My eyes closed. "Hmmm?"

"We're more than naked friends, you know."

"I know," I mumbled. "Naked friends don't spend holidays together. Naked friends don't leave clothes at each other's places."

"You gave me a drawer. Sort of."

"I just got out of a two-year relationship," I said, "Can we just keep doing what we're doing?"

"You mean we're just going to go on pretending you're using me for my incredible spooning skills, and I'm using you for—"

"Comic relief?"

"You ever think of doing standup?" he teased. "You'd be good at it."

"Yeah," I huffed. "I'm a source of endless entertainment."

"Might as well try and make money from it."

"Let's go to sleep."

"Okay. Assume the spoon!"

"Come back anytime," Nancy said, giving me a hug. "Really. Feel free to come back without Aidan."

"Mom," Aidan said with a grin and a shake of his head. He looked at me and smiled, "Told you they'd like you better than they like me."

With a final wave, we got into Janet's car. We had to get back to the city, back to reality. I had to work Black Friday at a restaurant in New York City.

Oh, the dread.

Aidan and I parted at Grand Central. I was planning on chastely kissing him goodbye, but he had other ideas. He wrapped me in his arms and dipped me, old Hollywood style.

"What are you doing?" I squeaked.

"Kissing you goodbye," he said. "Duh."

"Aidan—"

"The sooner you kiss me, the sooner I stop making a spectacle."

I had no choice but to pucker up and give it my all. Three hours later, when I walked into Antonio's, I still felt like I was walking on clouds and I was smiling like an idiot.

Jess embraced me. "Welcome back!"

"Thank you."

"You look almost back to normal."

I removed my glasses so I could show her the sickly bruises that still circled my eyes.

"Okay, I take it back."

A few hours later, the closers came onto the floor. I saw Zeb at the back computer by the kitchen, tying his apron and talking to a few of the support staff members. I approached him, wanting to find out about his Thanksgiving.

The look he gave me froze me in my tracks. He gestured with his head to the alcove near the back room. There was no one in my section so I followed him.

"I saw you," he said without preamble. "At Grand Central. With Aidan."

It felt like the floor shook beneath me. I pressed a hand to the brick wall to steady myself. I'd never been a good liar. I'd gotten C's in all my acting classes for a reason.

"I knew it," he said. "The night of my birthday—you made it seem like it was nothing."

"Okay, listen—"

Katrina came around the corner, looking tall and Russian. "What is happen? You have party without me? Everyone has party without me."

I managed a weak smile and ducked out back onto the main floor, Zeb not far behind me. "Drinks? After work?" I pleaded.

He paused a moment, then nodded before departing.

I was about to face the jury of Zeb, but I worried I'd already been sentenced.

169

"Table fifty is complaining about me to Jess," I said to Natalie. My first night back had to be a trial, really? I couldn't just have a seamless night?

"What are they saying?" Natalie took the tongs from the bar and plopped a lime into a vodka tonic.

"They're saying I rushed them."

"Did you?"

"I got a note that it was one of the girl's birthday dinner. I dropped dessert menus, let them sit, and then asked if they wanted anything. They said no. I asked if they wanted coffee. They said no. I asked if they wanted any more drinks. They said no. So, I dropped the check. And then they called Jess over."

Natalie rolled her eyes.

"It gets worse."

"How does it get worse?"

"One of the girls just put on a tiara."

"Birthday Bitch."

When Jess finished talking to the uppity table, she found me at the bar. "We're sending a free dessert."

"*What?*" I demanded. "Why? They didn't even order their own dessert! Why do we reward people for bad behavior?"

"Ever hear of Yelp?" Jess asked. "We're giving them an eight-dollar dessert in hopes that it buys us a little good will instead of a negative review."

I shook my head. "I so don't get this industry."

"If I got the spaghetti Carbonara without the egg, what will it be like?"

Oy.

"Salty bacon…in salty pasta," I said slowly.

The woman paused and then said, "I'll have the gnocchi."

"Any food allergies?" I asked her while gathering up the menus.

"Uh, why?"

"So I don't accidentally kill you." I could tell that she didn't know if I was being serious or not.

I waited.

"No, no food allergies."

"Glad to hear it."

Zeb and I went to a dark wine bar far away from Anto-nio's so I could spill.

My friend looked at me and said, "You lied to me."

"Yes."

"Why?"

"Uhm, wasn't it you who said no one in a restaurant could keep a secret?"

He had the grace to give a bit. "I might have said that. Have you told anyone?"

"No."

"How did this start? When did it start? The night of my birthday?"

I shook my head and recounted how I originally met Aidan. "I spent Thanksgiving with him and his family Upstate."

"That's kind of serious."

"No," I denied. "Not serious."

"Whatever you say," Zeb said. "I'm amazed. I never would've guessed you guys were together. Not by how you act at work."

"Well, I made it very clear that I was not okay having my dirty business paraded all around the restaurant. I don't know a lot, but I do know that having us outed as a couple is not something I want. Not there."

Couple. Huh. Interesting word choice, Sibby.

"I didn't tell you because…well, I'm still new and I know we're friends, but I just didn't know—"

"If you could trust me," he finished. "I got it. Still sucks though. Knowing I was right and that you lied to my face."

"Yeah, sorry about that."

We were silent for a moment over our glasses of wine. "What's he like—outside work, I mean?"

"Do you mean out of his clothes or—" I grinned.

"No! I mean, yes, I'm dying to know."

"He's," I paused, "great."

"Great? That's it. That's all you'll give me?"

I shrugged. "Sorry, Zeb. I'm not drunk enough to tell you, and besides, I never spoon and tell."

Chapter 15

Gabbagol [gah-ba-goll]:

    1. Capicola. (I think that's what he meant to say.) Coppa. Cured meat made from pork shoulder.

    2. Not Italian. Not English, either. Can you point to that on the menu, please?

    "Zeb knows," I said to Aidan that night when we were in bed. "But you have to pretend you don't know that he knows."

    "You are a giant migraine waiting to happen."

    I pinched his side.

    "Ow! How does he know?" he asked.

"He saw us in Grand Central."

"Ah."

"He won't tell anyone," I assured.

"Right."

"He promised."

"Drunk promises don't count."

"How did you know we were drunk?"

He sighed, sat up, and flipped on the bedside lamp. "We have to tell Jess."

"Why?"

"Because she's going to find out. Now that Zeb knows, it's only a matter of time before the whole staff knows."

"You don't trust him?"

"It's not about trust," he said.

"Then what's the problem?"

"The problem is, shit has a way of coming out."

"We agreed to keep this a secret," I said.

"That was more of you wanting to keep it a secret than me. And now you told Zeb."

"I didn't tell him—he saw us. Besides I'd rather quit than have a sit down with Jess about it."

"You don't mean that."

I nodded. "I *do* mean that. I'm not going to have our…relationship on display, or have it put into a box where the words *sexual harassment* are thrown around. This could turn into a thing. I could get fired. *You* could get fired."

"Sibby, there's not a no-dating policy at Antonio's. Look at Zeb and Kirk."

I stared at him. "You know about them?"

"They were all over each other at his birthday party. Obnoxiously so."

"They're co-workers. No one outranks the other one." I sighed. "I'll go in tomorrow and quit."

"It's the holidays, you're going to leave us in a lurch if you do that."

"And what's the other option, Aidan? We stop seeing each other." As soon as I said it, I knew that wouldn't fly with me. By the look on his face, I knew that wouldn't fly with him either.

"We're not going to agree on this, are we?" he said, sighing in temporary defeat.

"Nope. We don't have to do anything. Nothing has to change."

"Sibby?"

"Yeah?"

He winced. "Can you stop digging your nails into my leg? You've made your point."

I released him instantly. "Sorry."

"Why is it so important to you that we keep this a secret?"

"Why is it so important to you that we tell everyone?" I shot back.

We sat in silence.

Annie slathered her hash browns with Tabasco, onions, and jalapeños. Iron stomach, that one. I took a sip of weak diner coffee before I said, "I should just quit. Find another job."

"Why? Why not just tell the GM about you guys? It's not a big deal."

"It *is* a big deal."

"Why? I don't understand."

"Men who screw around in the workplace are treated differently than women who screw around in the workplace. Not to mention the fact that Aidan is technically my boss. It would be different if he was another server or a bartender, but he's got the power to fire me. If my co-workers knew we were dating, they'd give me a lot of crap. I'd lose their respect, and what happens if people start to think Aidan is treating me differently than them? I like my job. I like my co-workers. I don't want the dynamic to change."

"This was supposed to be a temporary job," she pointed out.

"It still is."

"Well, you sound like you really like it."

"I like it better than the office environment. Do you like your job? Does anyone actually like their job?"

Annie laughed. "My job pays the bills and I'm technically a chef, so that's cool, I guess. Even though most of the time I make nothing but grilled chicken with vegetables. Heather is totally bipolar. One minute she's laughing with me, the next she's blaming me for open wine going bad. It's exhausting."

"I know I'm supposed to have all this figured out," I said, "but I just have no idea what I'm doing. It's like I'm drunkenly staggering through my twenties."

"I think that's what you're supposed to do in your twenties."

"Well, great. Glad to know I'm right where I should be," I said with ironic bitterness. "But this can't continue into my thirties. Not having life figured out in your twenties is something people understand. But not having life figured out in your thirties? People will wonder where it all went wrong."

"Uhm, Sib, you're twenty-seven. Thirty is still years away."

"You know in New York, you blink and three years goes by."

"That's true."

"How do you hold it all together, Annie?"

She took another bite of spicy hash browns and swallowed them before answering. "I drink. A lot."

"Seriously."

"I am being serious. Do you know how annoyed I am that I decided to go to college and then culinary school? Where would I be if I'd known all along that I wanted to be a chef?"

"You wouldn't have met me," I said. "We never would've lived down the hall from each other freshman year at UNC and you never would've taken me to my first party."

"Where you never would've started your long-term affair with Jose Cuervo," Annie said with a grin. "Think of where you'd be without him."

I laughed. "I don't want to think about that."

"How's the book writing going?" Annie asked.

"It's not sounding the way I want it to sound," I answered.

"What do you mean? Is it corny enough?"

I nodded. "Yeah, the *schmaltz* factor is all there." I threw out the Yiddish word and knew I wouldn't have to clarify it for Annie. She'd been living in New York long enough—and been friends with me for years.

"Then what's the problem?"

"I don't know. It's funny."

"What's funny?" She frowned in confusion.

"The book," I explained.

"Funny like, you're cracking jokes in it?"

"Funny, like it's a parody."

"Huh."

"Yeah. I can't help it."

"So you're writing a comedy?"

"Inadvertently."

"Huh," she said again.

"Yeah. And I'm making the euphemisms really ridiculous. Like, over the top."

"So, go with it," she said.

"I think I have to."

"When do I get to read it?"

"When I know how I feel about it," I answered. "I make myself laugh writing it. That's a good sign, right?"

"How should I know? I'm the chef, you're the writer."

Natalie and I were in the main dining room, watching a family of five—three of them children—make a ruckus. The parents yelled at their eight-year-old who couldn't sit still. The toddler was watching a movie on an iPad at full volume, and the teenage girl sulked and brooded and refused to remove her ear buds while simultaneously singing along to terrible pop music.

"I swear the hostesses are seating them all in my section on purpose," I said.

"You have been getting a lot of kids lately," Natalie said.

"Last night, I had a family table thank me for tolerating them. Maybe they should rethink going out all together and not inflict themselves on unsuspecting waitresses. They let their kids dump out sugar caddies. I had to bring out the broom and dust pan."

"Oh, yeah. I've had a few of those."

"Please take them for me," I begged.

"Ha! What will you give me?"

"Muffins. Lots and lots of muffins."

"I'm not eating gluten. I'm on the Paleo diet."

I glared at her. "Damn you and your will power."

The eight-year-old started throwing a temper tantrum, tossing the large menu onto the floor. I shot Natalie a pleading look. "Have mercy! Have mercy!"

She sighed. "Fine. I'll take them. You take the next table of mine that comes in, okay?"

"Yes, yes, anything. You're a goddess!"

"You're laying it on a little thick, but I'm glad I'm appreciated."

Natalie slapped a serene smile on her face and approached the pandemonium. Twenty minutes later, the table was quiet, everyone munching away.

"How did you do that?" I demanded, in awe of Natalie's magical powers.

"I was openly sympathetic to the parents, I brought them bread immediately, and I complimented the teenager." She shrugged. "Oh, look you got a new table."

I turned and tried not to grimace. A table of ten.

Six of them were kids.

"Hi, how are you this evening?" I greeted my new party of four. All adults, two couples who reminded me of my parents, almost clones of each other. Thank goodness, no children. The Clones would be easy to deal with.

"Are you taking care of us tonight?" One of the Clones asked. He had a gray mustache and no hair on his head.

"I am."

"Jack, she looks like that actress we like. What's her name again?" Jack's wife studied me as she inquired.

"Sarah Silverman?" I asked.

Jack shook his head. "That's not it."

"Lisa Loeb?"

"Who?" Jack's wife asked.

"Musician," I clarified. "But I'm guessing no. How about Zooey Deschanel?"

"She's adorable!" Jack's friend said.

"Not the one I'm thinking of," Jack answered and I deflated.

I really wanted it to be Zooey Deschanel.

"She played Sarah Palin on SNL," Jack's wife said to her husband.

"Tina Fey!" I said suddenly.

"That's the one!" Jack said, smiling, making his

mustache dance across his face. "You must be really funny."

I smiled. "Inappropriately so."

"Anything to drink?" I asked the table of four obviously wealthy, mid-thirties businesswomen.

"Do I want the sangria?" one woman asked.

"If you want a hangover in your teeth," I said.

"Uhm, no. Vodka soda then, please."

"House red."

"House white."

I glanced at the last woman. "For you, ma'am?"

"I'm pregnant."

She looked like she was waiting for me to say something. I didn't know what to offer her, except for a belated, "Congratulations?"

She beamed.

"So, no drink?" I went on.

"How about a mocktail?" her friend suggested.

"What's a mocktail?" I asked before my brain could silence my mouth.

They looked at me like I was an idiot. The pregnant woman enlightened me. "A mix of fruit juices and club soda. Makes it a spritzer."

"Oh. Okay. So, you…want a…mocktail."

"Yeah. What fruit juices do you have?"

"Cranberry, pineapple, orange, grapefruit, and pomegranate," I listed.

"Oh! How about a combination of all of those, and a splash of club soda on top."

"That sounds *so* good!" one of her other friends chimed.

I wanted to kill myself, but I forced a smile. "Sure thing." I went to the bar and asked Tracksuit for all the juices.

"What do you mean? Like, a glass of each?" he demanded.

"No, like, all of them. In *one* glass…"

"Fuck my life," he muttered. "See the couple at the end of the bar? They're fighting."

"Anything good?" I asked.

He nodded again, more vigorously this time, his perfectly gelled hair not moving.

I took my sweet time getting my drinks together, shamelessly listening to the disgruntled couple. They were in their late thirties, overly tan, wasted, and had thick Jersey accents.

Hello, Bridge and Tunnel.

The woman was annoyed with the man, and doing nothing to keep that fact hidden. "What did you say to your friends?" she demanded at full volume.

He shrugged, looking like a sullen teenager. "We were at brunch. The guys asked if your pussy was tight and I said no."

"*You whaaat?!*" she shrieked, grabbing her purse and coat from beneath the bar. I thought she was going to leave, but before she departed, she stopped just long enough to punch the guy square in the nose and stomp out.

The guy nearly fell off his stool, and as he attempted to

go after her, I heard her say, "Fuck, I broke a nail."

Tracksuit and I stared at each other in total shock.

"I love my job," Tracksuit stated.

I took the drinks to the table of ladies and they all looked at me expectantly. "What happened at the bar?" the pregnant woman asked me.

I shrugged. "Don't ask me. I just work here."

Chapter 16

Tiramisu [tir-ah-me-soo]:

1. Italian for *a pick me up*. A layered dessert consisting of ladyfingers dipped in Marsala and espresso, then slathered with mascarpone. Sprinkled lightly with cocoa as a garnish.

2. It tastes *wet*. I don't… What? Veto.

Almost. Through. The night.

I tapped my pen on my server book while I waited for the two guys to order.

"What's that noise?" the young man asked.

"What noise?" I said, gently turning my body away

from him. I fiddled with the outline of my phone through my apron, but I couldn't find a way to silence it.

"It sounds like…the Speed Racer theme song?"

His friend laughed. "Yeah, I hear it too."

"It's your ring tone, isn't it?" the young man asked.

"Maybe?"

They laughed.

"I'm really sorry," I said. "I forgot to turn it off. I'm on call this weekend. Hospital," I joked. Thankfully, they were already on their second round of cocktails and laughed. I breathed a sigh of relief when my phone stopped ringing and their laughter continued. I discreetly left the table, heading towards the coffee station.

"Please tell me that wasn't your phone ringing," Aidan said as he pulled an espresso shot.

"Okay, that wasn't my phone ringing."

"You're not supposed to have your phone on the floor."

"Everyone else has their phone on them," I pointed out.

"No one else forgets to turn their phone on silent." He held out his hand and I sighed, reached into my apron pocket and gave it to him. "If you're nice to me, you'll get it back by the end of the shift."

"Hold on," I said, taking back the phone so quickly, he almost dropped his espresso. I shut my cell off. "There. Now you won't see if I get any really embarrassing texts from Annie."

"What's going on?" Natalie asked.

"Gah!" I jumped. "Don't do that."

"Do what?" She frowned.

"Move like an Asian ninja."

"As opposed to a Jewish ninja?"

I rolled my eyes.

"Why are you taking Sibby's cell phone?" Nat asked Aidan.

"Because it rings at tables," Aidan stated, grabbing my phone back from me and sticking it in his pants pocket.

"Which ring tone was it this time?" Natalie asked, not looking at all impressed. I shot her a look. "Flintstones? Jetsons?"

"It's happened more than once?" Aidan slowly turned his eyes to me.

"No," I said, dismissing him with my hand. "Okay— maybe—yes. Thanks, Nat."

"Anytime!" she chirped.

"It was the Speed Racer theme song," I muttered.

"What are you, eight?" Aidan asked.

"My table thought it was funny."

"Table sixty-two?" Natalie asked. "They're hammered. They think the bread basket is funny when you wear it as a hat."

"Why do you say that?" I asked.

She pointed. "Because one of them is wearing it as a hat."

"Be glad we have bigger problems at the moment," Aidan said, moving towards the table that was starting to draw attention.

"Watch my station a minute?" Natalie asked.

"Sure. Where are you going?"

"To the bathroom. I have to answer a text."

"I'll have an Irish Coffee," the barely twenty-one-year-old dude said.

"Sure. Would you like whipped cream?"

He frowned. "Irish Coffee doesn't usually have whipped cream."

"We serve our Irish Coffees with whipped cream, but you don't have to get it. Or I can put it on the side."

"No, that's okay. I'll just take the Bailey's and coffee."

"Wait, so you want Bailey's and coffee?" I asked in clarification.

"Yeah, an Irish Coffee, the normal way, like I said."

"Sir, Irish Coffee is *Irish whiskey*, coffee, and in most restaurants it comes with whipped cream."

"Then what's Bailey's and coffee?" he demanded.

"Bailey's and coffee."

He paused to think. "I guess I'll have Bailey's and coffee, then."

"Great. So, would you like whipped cream?"

"Are you going to give me my phone back?" I asked Aidan at the end of my shift.

"If you ask me nicely."

I fluttered my eyelashes. "Please, may I have my phone back?"

"Don't do that."

"Do what?"

"Flirt. You don't want me to flirt with you, so you're not allowed to flirt with me."

I frowned. "You're not making any sense. And not making sense is usually my job. So stop it. It's freakin' me out."

Aidan dug into his pocket and handed me my phone. "You wanna stay at my place tonight?" he asked.

"Shhh," I said, looking around to make sure no one could hear our conversation.

"Sibby," he growled. "I hate this."

"I'll make it up to you," I promised quickly.

"How?"

"You like fudge."

"I'm sick of fudge."

I raised an eyebrow. "Not with the way I'm thinking of eating it." I had the pleasure of watching Aidan blush— ever so slightly. I made a grown man blush. I leaned in to whisper, "My place. One hour."

I woke up congested and a little spacey. There had been a brief snap of decent weather in the city, and whenever that happened, my body didn't know what the hell was going on.

"You should call out of work," Aidan said.

"I can't." I drank the shot of daytime cold medicine, feeling like my head was about to explode.

"Yes, you can. You call out, then I spend the day taking care of you."

I shook my head. "No. You go home. Escape the Plague before I take you down with me."

"Sibby, it's okay to be sick and call out."

"I don't feel that bad," I said. "Honestly."

"Whatever you say. Want me to make you a cup of tea?"

"Okay."

Two hours later, we trekked to the train so I could go to work and Aidan could go home. I walked into Antonio's, riffling through my bag for cold medicine gel caps. Maybe I should've taken Aidan's advice and called out, but I didn't want to be a wimp.

"Ah, jackpot," I said, finding the meds at the bottom of my purse.

"You feel okay?" Zeb asked.

I swallowed a few capsules and then answered. "I have a little cold."

He frowned. "Are you sure? It doesn't sound little."

"Well it's not like it's the Swine Flu. Can Jews even get the Swine Flu?"

"I don't know, I'm not a doctor. You're so congested you sound like a cartoon character."

I perked up. "Thanks!"

"It wasn't a compliment."

"Well, I choose to take it that way. I took some medicine. I should be fine."

Fifteen minutes later, I was back upstairs, on the floor and ready for action. Zeb peered at me and then nudged me towards the new table. "Okay, team player, batter up. Let's see how you interact with real people."

I headed towards the only table in the restaurant. "How old is the Baby Amarone?" the middle-aged-man asked.

"It's a teenager," I said without pausing.

He smiled. "I'm good with that."

Maybe I could do this today after all.

As I punched in their order, Jess came onto the floor looking a bit frazzled. "You ever think she's just going to explode one day? I mean, where does she put all that espresso?" Zeb asked.

Jess overheard Zeb talking about her and smiled tightly. "Not now, Zeb. We've got a VIP, PITA on the way."

"PITA? You're expecting a falafel for dinner?" I asked.

"Pain in the ass," Zeb explained.

"Oh. Clever."

"What's wrong with you? Have you been drinking the Kool-Aid?" Jess demanded, looking at me.

"No, just cold medicine."

"Greeaaat," Jess said sarcastically. She glanced at Zeb. "You have to take the table."

"Who is it?" Zeb said.

"You'll recognize him, trust me."

"Someone famous, right?" Zeb said.

"Yep," Jess answered. "He comes in all the time."

"Oh, I know who you're talking about. I've waited on him before. To be fair, it's not usually him that's the issue— it's the date he brings," Zeb said.

An hour later, I was at the service station when the

famous actor came into the restaurant, his hand at the waist of some tall, waif model.

After Zeb brought Famous Actor a bottle of sparkling water, he said to me, "I have to use the restroom. I'll be two seconds."

"What if he wants to order?" I whispered.

"He won't be ready," he said. "He takes a while." With that last note, he slipped off to the bathroom and I dropped dessert menus at one of my tables.

"Is that who I think it is?" the young woman asked me as she pointed to Famous Actor.

"Who?" I asked, pretending to look around. "Oh. No, it's not. Does look like him though."

"You sure?" she pressed. "The resemblance is uncanny."

"I'm sure."

"Where are your mixed berries from?" the guy she was with asked.

"They're harvested by dwarves in Fairyland by the light of a silver sickle moon," I said as though I was completely serious. The guy just looked at me.

"Um, California," I said when he didn't laugh at my terrible joke.

I let the couple sit with their dessert menus another minute and was about to go talk to Tracksuit, but Famous Actor caught my eye and he smiled.

And like a stupid lapdog, I went to him.

"Did you need something?" I asked.

"We're ready to order," he said. "If you're ready."

"If you're ready, I'm ready," I said, pulling out my dupe pad and pen. Unfortunately the pen I reached for fell out of my hand, skittering across the floor. I sighed, but didn't reach down to pick it up. I pulled out another pen and waited, turning my attention to The Waif.

192

"I'm a vegetarian," she said.

"Okay..."

"And I have a lot of dietary restrictions."

"Ooooo-kay," I drawled.

A model with dietary restrictions.

Shocker.

After she listed all the things she *couldn't* have, I told her the two items on our menu she *could* have. That's right, two. Not five or seven.

Two.

She gave a sultry pout, handed me her menu, and then proceeded to order something that wasn't on the menu.

"Would you like something to drink?"

"No, just more limes for the sparkling water."

"All right. And for you, sir?" I asked. God, he was really attractive. No longer just the pretty boy in chick flicks, but a man who'd come into his own as a talented actor. I'd tell him that too, if I could just find my tongue.

"Surprise me," he said with a smile.

"Huh?"

"Surprise me," he said again. "Your favorites. Appetizer, entree, glass of wine."

"No restrictions?"

"No restrictions," he said.

I took his menu and thought for a brief moment about professing my undying love to him, but closed my mouth and nodded instead. Zeb waited for me at the computer by the kitchen. I nudged him out of the way so I could punch in their order.

"I took their order."

"Yeah, I saw that, but why? I was just in the restroom. I would've been back eventually."

"Zeb, it's a pooled house, and you guys just got done telling me his date is a pain in the ass. I thought I was doing you a favor. Anyway, since I have their order maybe we don't switch servers on them now that it's done, yeah?"

Zeb nodded. "Good luck."

"Now, if you'll excuse me, I have to go clarify to the kitchen what she ordered, and listen to Julian complain about how she is ruining his culinary genius by making up her own entree."

As their appetizers hit the table, I rushed to the bar for Famous Actor's glass of wine.

"How is everything?" I asked as I approached their table with the wine.

The Waif said nothing as she stirred limp kale around her plate with a fork.

"What am I eating?" Famous Actor asked.

"Artichokes alla Romana."

"Fuckin' good artichokes," he said.

"Glad you like—ahhhh!" My foot slid on the errant pen that I had failed to pick up earlier during their ordering process. I went sliding, trying to right myself, but it was no use.

The tray went up, I went down, and a freshly poured full glass of wine went all over Famous Actor.

"That could've happened to anyone," Zeb said, trying to contain his laughter.

"Yeah, but it didn't," I muttered, taking a sip of my hot

toddy. It was more toddy than hot and the cold medicine had long since run its course. I was having a quick drink and then had to go home and sleep off the headache.

"He found it funny. He's got a good sense of humor."

"His model girlfriend is another story," I pointed out.

"Not girlfriend, date."

"How do you know who he's dating?"

"*US Weekly*, duh."

"What's wrong with Sibby?" Johnny asked. Johnny, as in owner of Johnny's. He worked the bar a few nights a week, and when I'd started at Antonio's Zeb had introduced me to the entire staff at Johnny's, including the owner.

"She spilled an entire glass of wine on someone really famous. Like, really, really famous."

"No shit?"

I moaned.

"Guy was cool about it," Zeb went on. "So I don't know what her deal is."

"I should've called out sick," I said. "Drugs are the devil."

"You aren't really going to try and blame your clumsiness on cold medicine, are you? Drink more—it will help all your problems go away." Johnny pushed my hot toddy closer to me.

While I nursed my drink, I pulled out my phone, knowing what I was doing was dangerous, but I didn't care. I had spilled wine all over Famous Actor. I needed a pick-me-up.

I texted Aidan to see if he could meet me. He replied almost instantly and said he was already in the area with Caleb.

"You ready to go?" I asked Zeb.

"Sure."

We paid our bar tab and waved goodbye to Johnny.

"You gonna be okay getting home?" he asked.

"Yeah, I'm meeting Aidan. He'll see me home okay."

Zeb and I parted ways and then I met Aidan at the corner of 15th and 5th.

We walked towards Union Square, hand-in-hand. I wanted to be home, curled up in bed, snuggled under blankets and not thinking at all about wine and Famous Actor.

"Where's Caleb?" I asked.

"He went home."

"Why didn't you go with him?" I asked.

"I had a feeling you'd want me to come home with you."

"Did you happen to be waiting for me to get off work, hanging out in the area on purpose?"

"No... Maybe. Did you have an okay night?"

"I spilled wine all over a really famous movie star."

"No you didn't." He smiled in disbelief. "No fucking way. Which one?"

"It's not important and I don't want to talk about it, please."

He shook his head, like he couldn't believe it. "Is that why you texted me? You wanted me to make you feel better?"

"Maybe," I said, throwing that word back at him.

He looked at me while I dug around my purse for my wallet. I took out my Metro card and slid through the turn style.

"Thanks for waiting around for me," I said.

"You're welcome."

I heard the approach of the oncoming train, followed by the whoosh of air in my face as it glided on the tracks to a stop. The doors chimed open and we entered the relatively empty subway car. We sat down, and once we were on our way I finally spoke. "I was thinking I could make you a key."

"A key? Really?"

"Really."

"Sibby, look at me."

I did as he commanded. His blue eyes were warm and soft. Like blue chocolate chip cookies right out of the oven. Damn, I wasn't making any sort of sense.

"I didn't ask for a key."

"I know. I want you to have it."

He was quiet a moment and then he smiled. "Okay, make me a key."

I let out a breath. "This is very adult of us."

"Very," he agreed.

I closed my eyes and leaned my head against his shoulder. "I can't wait to be home in my Care Bear pajamas."

"Adult moment over."

Chapter 17

Fiori di Zucca [fee-or-ee deh zuk-ah]

    1. Zucchini blossoms stuffed with Italian cheeses, battered, and fried.

    2. Holy shit balls. More, please.

I walked up to the host stand holding a David's Bridal shopping bag. "A woman at one of my tables forgot this," I said, handing it to Aidan. "She just left."

"Go after her. You can probably still catch her," he said.

"She was snooty when I asked what she wanted to drink, and she didn't tip well. I'm not chasing after her for nothin'. Besides, it's raining and she's probably a Bridezilla."

Aidan chuckled. "Just put it there." I set the bag next to the host stand and then went back onto the floor.

I walked back onto the floor and approached the table of mid-twenty something hippies. "Would you guys like dessert? Coffee?"

"I'll have a coffee," the guy with the man bun said. "With soy milk."

"Oh, I'm sorry. We don't have soy milk."

"Almond milk?" Man Bun asked hopefully.

"Uh, no."

"What do you have besides regular milk?" he asked.

"Cream."

He sighed. "Black coffee will be fine."

I scooped up the dessert menus and headed to the computer, shaking my head.

"What?" Zeb asked.

"I don't get people."

"Who wanted what?"

"Man Bun over there wanted soy milk with his coffee."

He chuckled. "Did you just call him Man Bun? Tell him there's a Starbucks right around the corner."

"This is the problem with choices," I said. "Soy milk, almond milk, rice milk, half and half, cream, whole, two percent, one percent, skim… No one needs all those choices!"

"You forgot goat milk."

"Shut up."

He playfully shoved my arm. "I thought getting laid on a regular basis would improve your mood."

"Who's getting laid on a regular basis?" Natalie asked, passing us with a tray full of drinks.

"No one," Zeb and I said at the same time. I waited for Natalie to head off to her table before I glared at Zeb.

"Sorry," he said, sounding sincere.

"This shit is gonna blow up in my face," I said. "Isn't it?"

"Probably. It's your life's default."

"Libby! Libby…Libby, Libby!" the woman called over and over.

Who was she talking to?

"I think she means you," Nat said.

"Huh?" I asked, looking around. My gaze landed on the woman sitting by herself, holding a near empty glass of wine, which she waved at me. Holding in a sigh, I went to her.

"There you are, Libby. How many times do I have to yell your name?" she demanded.

"My name is Sibby."

"Excuse me?"

"Sibby. With an S. My name is Sibby, not Libby."

"I could've sworn you said your name was Libby."

"Okay, but it's not." We stared at each other for a moment. "Sooooo, can I get you something?"

She didn't reply as she set down her wine glass and reached for her purse, which rested on the chair next to her. Pulling down the sides of her leather bag, she revealed a small, fluffy, white dog. She scooped him out of the bag and placed him on the chair, cooing and speaking to him in a language reserved for babies and cute puffy things. She tore herself away from her dog just long enough to look at me and say, "I need a glass bowl of room temperature water and a menu. Sir Worthington Proudfoot would like to choose his own dinner."

"Oh, uhm—"

"Is your chicken soy fed? He's allergic to soy."

Completely flustered, I said, "I—I'm so sorry, but you can't have a dog in the restaurant."

She looked at me with disdain. "Excuse me, but you *will* address him by his name. Sir Worthington Proudfoot is a member of Her Majesty's council! He demands respect!"

I didn't know what to say, so I kept my mouth shut.

Crazy Dog Lady pointed to her furry companion. "Apologize. To him. You hurt his feelings."

I looked down at Sir Worthington Proudfoot, who gazed up at me with deep brown eyes. He licked his nose and started panting.

"I'll be right back."

"He's hungry, so hurry!" Crazy Dog Lady called after me.

I went straight to Jess.

"You're making me dinner?" I asked as I walked

through the front door of my apartment. I'd been out running errands, and even though I knew Aidan was coming over, I was still surprised by his presence. It was the good kind of surprise. I'd had a rough week at the restaurant, what with Crazy Dog Lady.

Aidan began pulling out ingredients from the fridge. "Yep."

"I should've given you a key a long time ago," I stated.

He grinned, proud of himself. "Where is your biggest pot?" He started opening cabinets and leaving them open until he found what he was looking for.

"You're going to make a mess, aren't you?"

"Oh yeah."

The buzzer rang and I went to answer it. I pressed intercom. "Hello?"

"Surprise!" My mother's voice blared through the speaker. "I'm out here with your father."

I made some sort of garbled noise in the back of my throat. "What are you—what's—"

"You going to let us up, Wapa?"

I cringed at the childhood nickname. "Sure," I said, my breathing increasing almost to a rapid pant.

Panic attack.

I buzzed them up and then went into the kitchen. There was already spaghetti sauce on the floor and the smell of garlic in the air.

"Who was it? Amazon? Did you get a package?" Aidan asked.

"My parents."

Aidan's head whipped around and he nervously began to squeeze the meatballs he was forming.

"Uhm, Aidan? You're turning your meatballs into hamburger patties."

The knock on the door announced my parents' arrival. "What the hell am I supposed to do?" I demanded.

"Chillax, open a bottle of wine, and invite them to dinner."

"But you—and I—we're—ah crap!" I walked to the door and opened it. My mom squealed, and all five feet of her barreled into me, knocking me off balance. I winced when part of her collided with my nose. She pulled back to look at me.

"The nose doesn't look too bad," she said.

I looked at my dad. "You told her I broke my nose?"

He nodded. "Though I'm not sure I ever got the full story."

There was a clatter of pots and pans in the kitchen and my dad asked, "Is Matt cooking?"

"Aidan, can you come out here?" I asked, my voice tinged with hysteria. "And bring wine!"

"Why do they call you Wapa?" Aidan whispered.

"Later," I mumbled, though I had no intention of telling him.

My parents sat on the couch, looking shell-shocked. I started my story with the day I lost my job and ended around the time I broke my nose. My mother was the first to speak. "So that's what a brain aneurysm feels like."

I winced.

"I'm disappointed in you, kiddo," my dad said, taking a healthy slug of wine.

"I know. I know it looks like I failed—on many accounts but if you just—"

"I'm not talking about losing your job or about Matt cheating on you," my dad interrupted.

"You did go to the lady doctor, right? I mean to check and make sure everything—"

"Mom!" I hissed in embarrassment.

"Well, did you?" she demanded.

"Yes, okay? I did." My mom let out a breath and Aidan discreetly filled up all of our wine glasses, polishing off the last of the bottle.

"As I was saying"—my dad glared at Aidan, who still hadn't said anything except for introducing himself—"I'm disappointed in you. Why didn't you tell us the truth when all this happened?"

"Did you miss the part where I said I lost my job, got cheated on, *and* broke my nose? All in the span of four months? It's been a bit embarrassing."

"You forgot adding *got a new boyfriend* to that list," Mom said.

"That's not embarrassing," I assured Aidan.

"Sibby, we're your parents and we love you, no matter what. You should have told us," my mom went on.

"I know."

"We could've been there for you. Do you need money?" Dad asked.

"No, I'm good."

"And this restaurant you work in…" Mom looked like she was about to faint.

That was me. Sibby Goldstein, trying to kill her parents since birth.

"It's an Italian place," I said. "Been there forever. Neighborhood staple. Great people."

"And you're—happy?" My dad asked.

"Getting there," I said softly. "I'm a work in progress."

Halfway into our second bottle of wine, my parents were hammered and had moved into the kitchen. My mom was finishing Aidan's attempt at spaghetti and meatballs.

"Sorry, they don't drink a lot," I whispered to him. "Not unless you count *Manischewitz* wine spritzers."

Aidan grinned. "I really like your parents. Especially since your dad threatened to track down Matt and kick his ass."

"He'd have to pay someone to do it. My dad's a surgeon, his hands are everything."

"You know, this is not how I planned on meeting your parents for the first time."

"Oh, no? What did you have in mind?"

"Well, when we'd been dating for six months. *Publicly* dating for six months," he amended, "you would've asked me to come with you to Atlanta to meet your parents. This is after you told them all the stuff you'd been lying to them about."

I shook my head. "So weird, all this time I thought they'd be disappointed in me. I thought they'd think I was a failure."

"They don't think that. Only you think that."

I nudged his knee with mine and rested my head on his shoulder. "This is nice."

"Oh no! I burned the balls!" my mom wailed.

"It's okay," my dad soothed. "That's why they invented Chinese takeout."

Aidan looked at me with a huge grin. "Yep. I really like your parents."

"Whatever. At one of my sleepovers my mom told my friends she hoped for early menopause because she wanted to use her diaphragm as a Frisbee."

"She didn't say that," Aidan said in disbelief. "Did she?"

"I was twelve. It scarred me for life. Fault of the wine spritzers."

"Something is missing from the tables," I said, looking around the main dining room at Antonio's.

"Salt shakers," Natalie answered as she picked up a spotty knife, stuck it in her apron, and replaced it with another. "We're not putting salt shakers on the tables anymore."

"Why?"

Natalie grinned. "Do salt shakers need a reason not to be on the tables?"

"Yes."

"Some guy salted his own pasta too much, and then complained that it was too salty and sent it back, so now we don't keep salt on the tables."

"Oh sure, because why would we hold stupid people accountable for their stupidity," I grumbled.

She laughed. "What's with you?"

"My parents showed up unannounced in town."

I made my way to the coffee station and pulled an espresso. I needed a serious caffeine jolt. After Aidan and I had piled my drunken parents into a cab, he and I had split another bottle of wine.

"You're kidding. They just showed up unannounced?"

"Yep." I added a hefty dose of milk and sugar to my espresso and took a swallow. "I wound up explaining all the things that I had kept secret over the past few months."

Everything except that Aidan was my boss.

"How'd it go?"

"I got them drunk."

"Ah, sedated them for their pain?"

"Exactly."

"How'd they take the news?"

"Okay, I think. They're in town for a few days, so I'll be able to get a good read on them. Which reminds me, can we do some shift swapping so I can hang out with them?"

"Sure thing."

I tossed my empty sugar packets at the garbage can and missed. I crouched down to retrieve them.

"Your mom—do you look like her?"

"Yeah, but she's smaller than I am."

"Right. And your dad? Does he have really bushy eyebrows?"

I looked up at her. "Yeah. Did I show you a picture of them or something?"

Natalie shook her head. "Your parents. They're here."

"What!" I yelled.

My parents really needed to stop just showing up randomly.

"What's wrong?" Natalie asked as I was trying to move around her and run toward my parents.

"Hi, honey!" my mom chirped. She looked bright and happy and not at all like she'd had too many glasses of wine for her small frame.

"What are you guys doing here?" I demanded, a tight smile splayed across my face.

"We just wanted to see where you worked," my dad answered. "See if the food is as good as you said it was."

I felt my eye twitch.

I should never have told them where I worked. I should never have shown them how to Google things. This was my own fault, really.

"I need to tell you something," I said right as Whitney, the hostess joined us, holding two menus in her hands.

"I'll take those, thanks," I said, taking the menus from her. "Come on, I'll show you the courtyard." I needed to get them away from co-workers and Aidan, who was still downstairs doing inventory.

"Oh, this is so pretty!" my mom exclaimed, sitting down. "I love the stone floor. And look at that iron work!"

"Very nice," my dad commented.

"Okay, listen, there's something I didn't tell you last night."

"God, there's more?" Mom breathed. "Are you pregnant? Am I going to be a grandmother?"

"Stop! Gah! I'm not pregnant." I took a deep breath. "Okay, so you know I'm dating Aidan."

"Yes, we know," my dad clipped. Well, that clued me in on how Dad felt about Aidan. Aidan, who wasn't the cheater, but who would be blamed for all of the male species' shortcomings since he was dating my father's only daughter.

"He's the manager here." I'd lowered my voice since I saw Natalie lurking in the doorway of the courtyard room, wanting to come over to introduce herself. I shook my head at her and she shrugged and waited.

"You're dating your manager?!" Mom exclaimed far too loudly.

The twitch intensified. "Yes, but please keep it down. No one knows. So if you see him wandering around, pretend like you haven't met yet. Okay?"

"What kind of life are you leading?" Dad wondered aloud. "Are you a spy?"

I rolled my eyes. "Just promise me, okay?"

"I think we can figure out how to pretend," Mom answered.

"If you're lying to people about it, do you think you should be doing it?" my dad asked.

"We're in Antonio's. That sort of logic doesn't apply." I waved Natalie over. "Let me introduce you to some of my co-workers."

"So what's your next step?" Dad asked the next day. We were walking through the snow-covered ground of Central Park, headed toward the train to meet Mom and

Aidan at Katz's Deli in the Lower East Side. Nothing like a$22.45 sandwich.

Oy.

Dad wanted time alone with me first. It was inevitable, really. Better to get it over with.

"I don't know," I admitted. "I've got some ideas. Sort of."

"You going back to the office environment?"

I shook my head and hunched lower in my coat. "No. I know you hate the idea that I work in a restaurant—"

"I don't hate the idea," he cut me off. "I just don't want you to get stuck doing it."

"I was stuck in the office, I just didn't realize I was stuck. That's the thing; people don't get it, but they're actually trapped in their suits. Waiting tables is flexible and good money, and it's giving me time to figure out what I want to do and be creative..."

"You're being creative?"

"Yes."

"You're writing something?" he asked in surprise.

"Eh, I have an idea of something I'd like to write," I said evasively.

I couldn't quite bring myself to tell him I was writing a romance novel with thirty-one penis euphemisms in it.

Yes, I'd counted.

My father dropped the writing subject. "And this Aidan... You sure you should be seeing someone right on the heels of a breakup?"

"You didn't like Matt when you first met him. Though, now I'm thinking you were correct in your opinion of him."

"I can't believe that bastard did that to you."

"It's okay," I said.

"It's not."

"It is," I insisted. "Because if we're being honest, it needed to end. I can say that now, looking back."

"And this guy—"

"Aidan," I stressed. "Give him a chance. For me?"

"Okay, Wapa." He squeezed my shoulder.

We walked a few feet in silence before I said, "So, by the way, Matt's a homosexual."

Chapter 18

Burrata [boo-rah-tah]:

1. A fresh Italian cheese made from mozzarella and cream. The outer shell is solid mozzarella, while the inside contains both mozzarella and cream, giving it an unusual, soft texture.

2. I'd cut a bitch for burrata.

After four days, a Broadway show, and a few good meals, my parents were on a plane home. I was grateful for how they reacted to my entire life switcheroo. They had been invasive, but also totally supportive of me and my choices, and there hadn't been any guilt.

Surprisingly.

"How's the spaghetti and meatballs?" the guy asked, bringing me back to the present.

"Good," I answered carelessly.

"Is it better than the fettuccine and beef Bolognese?"

"No."

"Really?"

I held in a sigh. "Really."

"Hmmm. I just…don't…know…"

While I waited for him to make a seemingly impossible decision, my gaze wandered around the dining room. It was half-full with customers who'd already paid but didn't want to go out into the cold. Not that I blamed them. I'd worn long underwear under my jeans—long underwear that went up past my bellybutton.

"What to get, what to get…" the man went on.

"Harold, just choose something!" Harold's wife snapped.

"You can do two half orders," I said.

Harold looked at me like I'd just told him I'd give him a kidney. "Really? Oh my god, you're the best!"

I smiled and gathered up the huge menus after he'd chosen his two dishes. As I punched in the order, I saw another table being seated in the dining room. It was a couple in their late forties, and when the woman took off her coat, she revealed a microscopic, clingy dress that a twenty-year-old might wear on a night out clubbing. It was low cut, tight, and shiny.

"She does know it's ten degrees out, right?" Zeb asked me.

"If she asks for a hot water with lemon, I'm seriously going to hit her."

"I'm cold just looking at her."

"I'm embarrassed for her," I said. "I never wore those kinds of dresses, even when they *were* age appropriate."

"This is a family restaurant!" Zeb said, pretending to be scandalized. "I know they're in my section, but I can't take them. I'll say something I'll regret. They'll complain to Jess and I'm already on thin ice with her."

"Why?"

"I told her that bangs were not good for her face shape."

"God, we judge a lot."

"Think we should stop?"

"Nope. What would we do in our spare time?" I sighed. "Okay, rock, paper, scissors for who takes this table."

Zeb won, which meant I had to take the woman and her fake boobs. I spent fifteen minutes at the table, just taking the order.

"Thank you, thank you, thank you," Zeb said.

"You so owe me. And I quote: No butter, no oil, no salt, no garlic, no onions, no meat, no dairy."

"I'll buy you a Reese's Peanut Butter Cup."

I glanced over at the woman and caught a glimpse of a lotus flower tattoo on her spine as she adjusted her breasts to take a boob selfie. I looked at Zeb and raised an eyebrow.

"Okay. *Two* Reese's Peanut Butter Cups."

The holiday season came and went. Before I knew it, it was Valentine's Day. Another day, another shift. They all seemed to bleed together. The server nightmares were growing worse. There were many nights Aidan had to shake me awake because I was mumbling in my sleep. Apparently I answered menu questions to imaginary guests in Dreamland.

But the money and flexibility of the job were impossible to resist.

Before I knew it, it was March and the entire city was suffering from the late-winter blues. The staff at Antonio's had been having a difficult time faking happiness for the miserably cold customers who came through our doors each night.

I pushed away the empty plate of family meal and doodled on my dupe pad while we waited for the pre-shift meeting to start. The phones were ringing, and Jess jumped up every five seconds to answer them. Aidan had taken the lead, shuffling papers, and getting situated. His gaze lingered on me for one long moment, and Zeb nudged my ankle, but I pretended not to notice. Thankfully, Natalie was in her own little world and completely unaware.

"So," Aidan said, "before we go over the food, I want to read you guys an email that someone wrote in about their dining experience:

I had the pleasure of dining at Antonio's recently and I have to say, I've never been so happy. The food was delicious, the ambience warm and comfortable, but the reason for my exceptional dining experience was because of our server, Anastasia.

Anastasia expertly guided us through the extensive menu, helped us select a moderately priced wine, and she felt like an old friend who genuinely wanted us to enjoy ourselves. I will be back, and I'll tell everyone I know about how much I enjoyed my meal at Antonio's. Thanks, Anastasia! You are the best!"

"Anastasia?" Zeb smirked, refusing to look at me. "Who's Anastasia? No one here is named Anastasia."

"They probably meant Katrina," I said immediately. "Russian royalty, Russian waitress. Honest mistake."

Aidan looked at me when he said, "You know, this is not the first letter we've gotten about Anastasia. She's all over our Yelp reviews."

"You're kidding!" Zeb said, pulling out his phone and opening the Yelp app. He scrolled through the Antonio's reviews and started laughing. "Oh my God, this is hilarious. *If you go to Antonio's for dinner, make sure you sit in Anastasia's section. She's delightfully funny and honest about the food. It's like getting a one woman show.*"

"Can we talk about the specials?" Natalie asked. "So we can, you know, start setting up?"

Zeb and I looked at each other, wondering what had Nat in such a foul mood. She was never short tempered. She was sweet, so this was weird and out of character.

"Sure," Aidan said, not at all fazed.

A few hours later, I watched Natalie lose it at a table. I mean, full-on, did-she-cook-your- rabbit-yet lose it. While she was in the middle of her tirade, I went to her side, pasted a smile on my face, and looking at her customers said, "She's an actress and she's method acting." I pushed her toward the direction of the bathroom and then smoothed over the table's ruffled feathers with a round of drinks on the house and quickly took their orders.

"Watch my section a minute? Everyone's okay," I said to Zeb.

"I can't watch the whole dining room," Zeb said. "Where's Nat?"

"She had a bit of a freak out," I explained. "Just give me five minutes?"

"Fine. Go. Let it all burn down around me."

I ducked into the bathroom and called out, "Nat?" The door to one of the stalls opened, revealing Natalie sitting on the closed toilet, clutching a wad of toilet paper in her hand. Her eyes were red.

"I'm—"

"Not here," I interrupted. "Whatever it is, don't say it here."

She nodded.

"Pull yourself together," I commanded. "After work. You and me. Got it?" She nodded again, stood up and sniffed. I set my hand on her shoulder, and said gently, "Wash your face. Okay?"

"Okay," she whispered.

I headed back out onto the floor and Aidan was waiting for me, a look of concern on his face. "Is she okay?"

"I don't know. I'm going out with her after work."

"I'll be at your place."

I nodded. "Sounds good."

"Your table is flagging you down," he said.

"That's not a wave. I think she's having a seizure."

Aidan smiled and strolled away.

I waved back at the woman and yelled across the dining room, "I'll be right there!"

Natalie inhaled a shaky breath. "I'm…kind of…pregnant." She whispered her announcement, turning solemn eyes to the table. It was loud in the twenty-four-hour Latin diner and it covered the silence between us.

"I—you're—pregnant. Okay." I nodded. "I had no idea you were dating someone."

"It's new, and I wanted to see where it went before I told anyone."

"What are you going to do?"

"I really have no idea. Tad and I have only been dating for two months. I was still waiting for the other shoe to drop with him and now this happened."

"Have you told him yet?"

She shook her head. "Not yet. I wanted to be sure. What the fuck am I going to do?" she nearly wailed, placing her head in her hands.

"Oh, I am not so good with the life advice. I don't have crap figured out. I'm good with inappropriate comments. Can I offer you one of those?" I asked almost desperately.

"It wasn't supposed to be like this," Natalie said. "I wanted a 401K. I wanted to be married, and be a really hip New York mom. Now, I'm going to have to move to Jersey. And I really *hate* Jersey."

"Okay, listen," I said, taking her hand. "I had a 401K and a stable-ish boyfriend. That all went to shit overnight.

Life sucks sometimes, but the detours make it interesting, don't you think?"

She made a garbled noise and shrugged. "This detour is going to make me throw up for three months."

"Only if you're lucky—morning sickness can last longer than the first trimester."

She looked at me with questioning disdain.

"I read a lot," I explained.

"Can we talk about something else? Can you distract me, please?"

I blew out a puff of air and grasped at the only straw I had. "I'm sleeping with Aidan."

She nodded and swallowed. "That'll do."

The next afternoon, Aidan and I were enjoying a cozy moment on my couch. "What happened with Nat?"

"Can't tell you," I said.

"Why not?" Aidan demanded.

"Because it's not my secret to share," I said, not looking him in the eye.

"You so told her about us, didn't you?"

"No!" Pause. "Yes. But only because I was trying to make her feel better about the secret I can't tell you—so don't ask again. Unless—"

"Unless what?"

"We could do an exchange of information."

"I'm listening."

"Julian's cheerful mood has lasted. What's up with him?"

Aidan shook his head. "Can't say."

"Still?"

"Still." Aidan grinned and kissed me before getting up off the couch.

"Where are you going?"

"Home."

"Why?" I demanded.

"Because, as much as I love sitting on the couch and relaxing with you, I want to go out. And by go out, I mean I want to take you out."

"You mean, like, on a date?"

"Exactly, like on a date."

"But we don't do that," I protested.

"So let's start."

"No."

"Sibby… Your parents like me now, but what happens when you tell them we only order take out and spoon."

"Enough with the spooning jokes. We get it, you're a good spooner."

"You know spooning is a euphemism for—"

"Got it, thanks! And my dad doesn't like you."

"Yes, he does. We had a talk," Aidan responded.

"Huh? When?"

"The day before they left. We had a heart-to-heart. We're good."

I blinked stupidly. So much I didn't know.

"He invited me to next year's Passover Seder," Aidan went on. "Told me I just had to try gefilte fish. What *is* gefilte fish anyway?"

"Gelatinous, slimy…fish patties. The most disgusting Jewish food in the history of the world."

"It can't be that bad," he said, trying not to make a face. Not that I blamed him. The stuff made me dry heave.

"I used to give my share to my childhood dog under the table. Even he wouldn't eat it."

"Huh. Maybe your dad doesn't like me after all."

"Nah, he's a jokester. This is his way of indoctrinating you into the tribe. We'll just put a ton of horseradish on it and it will be okay."

"Why don't I believe you?"

I shrugged.

"He told me why they call you Wapa."

I moaned theatrically.

"So cute. Really. Little Wapa Bug!"

"Veto! You are *not* allowed to call me that."

He grinned. "So, I'll pick you up for dinner at seven o'clock."

"No," I stated. "We can't—I won't—"

"Nowhere on the West Side." Aidan amended. "Somewhere dark so no one will know that you're embarrassed to be seen with me."

"The East Village is good for that," I remarked with a smile. "And there's nothing embarrassing about you." I should've been parading him around, blasting Facebook with cute, disgusting photos of us that would make acquaintances jealous.

"I'll let you choose the place," he conceded. "We can even stay in Brooklyn if you want."

"Really? You want to take me on a date that badly?"

"Shocking, I know. God, you make me work really hard for it."

"Not anymore," I quipped.

He shook his head. "Seven o'clock."

"Fine. But you're not allowed to look cuter than me."

Aidan grinned and then left. When I had the place to myself, I called Natalie to check in with her. She didn't answer and I wondered if she was telling her new guy she was pregnant. My life had become dramatic by association —and my life was dramatic enough. Still, good friends were hard to come by.

But I'd take them, drama and all.

I took Aidan to a Polish restaurant in Greenpoint that had a name I couldn't spell or pronounce. All the wait-resses were dressed in traditional Polish serving attire, the walls were lined with animal heads, and the booths were large and wooden.

Nothing on the menu cost more than fifteen dollars, and we split a platter of kielbasa, pierogis, and other Polish specialties. We were on our second round of drinks when Aidan said, "I haven't seen Caleb in a week."

"Really?" I thought for a moment. "Come to think of it, I haven't seen Annie in a fair amount of time, either. She popped in for a quick lunch with my parents and me when they were in town, but that was it. Think she and Caleb are nesting?"

"Yeah, or doing it all the time."

"Uhm, ew."

"Guys don't nest," he explained. "You all make things pretty, cook us things, and add photos to the place, but dudes just leave their socks around their girlfriends' apartment."

"What else do they do?" I asked with a smile.

"Take out the trash, fix electronics, stuff like that."

"Manly."

"Yep. So, I know you can't tell me about Natalie's secret, and I won't ask again, but can you tell me… Who is Anastasia?"

Maybe it was the second beer, maybe it was because I was tired of holding on to a lot of secrets, but I blurted out, "My alter ego."

Aidan hid his smile, or tried to.

"Don't laugh at me."

"I'm not, I just…you're hilarious. You know that right?"

"According to Yelp reviews, Anastasia's a gas," I drawled.

"So why the need for an alter ego?"

I shrugged. "Remember Crazy Dog Lady?"

"The woman who kept calling you Libby? Yeah. I remember. Jess and I had a meeting about it."

"Wait, what? You did?"

"Yeah. We had a discussion about what to do if she ever came back—we won't let her eat with us again. There's funny crazy and then there's Crazy-Dog-Lady crazy."

"Good to know. Justice has prevailed!"

He cleared his throat. "So—Anastasia?"

"Right! After that woman, I refused to give out a real name. Customers now get a persona. I can't believe it's taken you this long to hear about it, actually. Everyone knows."

"*Everyone*, everyone?"

I nodded. "Even the hostesses. When they get requests

for people to sit in Anastasia's section, they don't bat an eye. They know it's me."

"Wow, I really should *maître d'* more. At least then I'd have an idea of what's going on. You know you can't do that, right?"

"Do what?"

"Lie."

"Of course I can."

"You can't, Sibby."

"Why not? When Julian tells us to push a dish that isn't good, we lie and tell the customers it's good and they should order it."

He sighed. "You make a valid point."

"Are you getting complaints about Anastasia?"

"No."

"Then what's the problem?"

"No problem, I guess."

"Pretending to be Anastasia makes me happy. And you want me to be happy, don't you?" I made my eyes wide and doe-like.

"Don't look at me that way."

"I'll bake you cookies if you keep my secret."

"I'm no match for your cookies."

"I'm a terrible mother," the woman at my table said.

"Look at my kids! They're fighting over the last Zeppole like they haven't eaten for a month."

The two kids had chocolate sauce all over their faces and powdered sugar on their clothes, and yet the mother stared at them both so fondly.

"I think you should have them fight to the death for it. Like gladiators!"

"Shhhh!" she stage-whispered. "Don't give them any ideas."

"I'll put five bucks on your little girl."

The woman glanced at her son, who had to be at least three years older than the six-year-old girl. "You sure?" The mother looked back at me. "You've got a bet!"

At that moment, the little girl stuck one of her fingers into her mouth and wet-willied her brother. When he dropped the zeppole back onto the plate to cover his ear, the girl snatched the dessert off the plate and stuffed it into her mouth before he could react.

Sometimes, I really liked my job.

Chapter 19

Barbaresco [bahr-bah-resk-oh]:

1. Red wine produced in the Piedmont region of Italy. Often compared with Barolo, but there are distinct differences between the two wines.

2. This is the part where we talk about *tannins*.

"Sir," I said calmly. "I can't do anything about that."

The middle-aged-man glared at me and held up his wine glass that was devoid of wine, but full of sediment. "This is outrageous."

"Sir, wine comes from grapes. Grapes come from

nature. That, right there, in your glass, is a little bit of nature."

Because he didn't find me humorous, he asked to speak to my manager.

Whine Guy. Definitely.

Sighing, I went in search of Aidan who was managing the floor that night.

"Aidan," I said when I found him in the courtyard room.

"What did you do?" he teased.

"Nothing. Well, not nothing." I shoved the glass of wine dirt at him. "My guest is blaming me for the sediment."

"Well, it is your fault. You stomped the grapes yourself, right?"

I raised an eyebrow. Aidan was flirting with me. Openly. "Have you been drinking?"

"What table," he said, ignoring my question.

"Thirty-three." I went to contend with a few of my other tables and was at the bar grabbing a second round of Cosmos for my Long Island ladies when I heard Aidan raise his voice at Whine Guy.

"You're going to blame my server for wine sediment in your glass? Seriously? That's like going to the dentist and blaming him for your cavities."

Guests turned to stare. I dropped off the Cosmos and then slid into a corner to watch the scene unfold. Whine Guy stood up, threw down some bills, grabbed his wife's hand, and stalked out. Aidan sighed, collected the money, and came over to me.

"God among men," I said.

"I hate seeing you mistreated," he said quietly, throwing a smile at my table of women. They raised their Cosmos in salute to him.

"Stop it," I said. "Stop being cute and amazing and perfect. At least at work."

"What will you give me?" he demanded.

I gave him a look and raised an eyebrow.

"God, if only there weren't cameras in the wine room," he muttered before turning away.

"Do you guys have any questions?" I asked.

"About the menu, or life?" the man wondered aloud.

"The menu. I don't know squat about life."

"Neither do we. We need therapy," the woman at the table joked.

"No worries. I need medication."

The woman pointed a finger at me. "I like you."

I smiled. "I like you. You guys have been the nicest table I've had all night."

The guy made a face. "Let me guess. The bar wasn't set too high, was it?"

"Not really," I joked.

Sort of.

The table ordered three courses and an expensive bottle of wine and then tipped very well. I wasn't so lucky with my next table.

"It was a pleasure meeting you," the father slurred, vigorously shaking my hand. "Oh my God, you have the tiniest hand in the entire world."

"Yeah, I have the hands of a child," I said with a strained smile.

The father looked at his twenty-something son. "You've got to feel her hand."

I reached out to shake the embarrassed son's palm. "That's…a nice hand," he said, smiling awkwardly.

"Have a good night!" I said, disentangling my grip.

"Did that really just happen?" Jess asked after the guests left.

"Yeah, I can't believe you overheard that."

"That's the best thing I've heard all night! Top five over all."

"I made top five? Sweet!"

"I have good news and I have bad news," Aidan said to me that night as he came into my apartment, using his shiny new key.

"What's the bad news?"

"Bad news is we're starting Sunday brunch. Julian bought waffle makers."

"Oh, God. Is this why Julian has been in such a good mood? He found a new way to torture servers?" Aidan shook his head. "I'm not going to like this next part, am I?"

He sighed. "You're our newest hire, which means you get stuck working brunch."

"You're kidding, right?"

"Nope. But you'll get really good breakfast food."

"Our Sunday brunches are sacred, Aidan. Now, instead of going to them, I have to work? This totally sucks." I sighed. "What's the good news?"

"The good news is I'm managing." He grinned. "We get to hang out together."

"What about the bartender and support staff?"

"Yeah, until there's enough business, it's just you, me, and a few kitchen guys."

"When does this start?" I demanded.

"This weekend. Cheer up. Just means more time with me."

That did cheer me up.

"Two tables in three hours," I said, beating my head against the bar. "This was a rotten idea."

Aidan grinned as he cleaned another bottle of liquor. "You get paid to hang out with me."

"Four dollars and fifteen cents an hour doesn't even cover taxes. This is bullshit."

He pulled out a deck of cards and tossed them in my direction.

"You've been holding out on me." I took the cards and shuffled them. "What should we play? Blackjack?"

"No fun unless you're betting," Aidan stated.

"I've never played Blackjack for money."

"You're kidding right? You've never been to Vegas? Or AC?"

"Nope," I responded.

"Oh, Sibby. Get out your bus pass, we're going to AC."

"I need a shiny gold track suit and blue silvery hair first."

"I know a guy."

"Yeah, it's Aaron." I laughed. "Okay, Gin it is."

"Little early for drinking, Sib."

"Pick up your cards, Aidan."

Another hour passed and I wondered how I was going to live through the slowness of the stupid brunch shift. Nothing was worse than being idle.

"You bitch when you're busy, and you bitch when you're slow," Aidan pointed out.

"Server way," I said. "Why did the owner think this was a good idea? We don't have drink specials, we're in a weird part of the city, and no one wants a heavy Italian meal at 11:00 a.m. Antonio's: the place where logic goes to die."

"You sound like Zeb."

"He was the one who told me that's the Antonio's motto."

He looked out the large glass windows at the front of the restaurant. "I think our boredom is about to be over."

"What makes you say that?" I asked, scooping up the cards.

"Wow, this place is dead!" Annie yelled into the empty dining room.

"Maybe Sibby should get on a table and dance, attract some people," Caleb suggested.

"What are you guys doing here?" I demanded, jumping up from the bar stool and hugging my best friend.

"Aidan's idea," Caleb said.

"Thought you might be bored." Annie grinned.

"You guys are kind of amazing," I stated.

Affronted, Aidan said, "What about me? It was my idea."

I pretended to bow down to him. "I'll worship you later."

"That's what I'm talking about." Aidan pulled out the glasses and fixings for Bloody Marys. "You guys take a seat and start drinking."

Four hours later, brunch was officially over and I had fifty bucks in my pocket to show for it. Caleb and Annie had stumbled out of Antonio's an hour earlier, blasted and rowdy.

"Your friend is an obnoxious drunk," I stated.

"Not as obnoxious as *your* friend," he said.

"At least they have each other to lean on," I commented.

"All in all, it wasn't that bad, was it?" he asked.

"I made fifty bucks."

"But you won the French toast eating contest and you got to hang out with me. We spoke in accents."

"I should never have told you we do that."

"Why?"

"Because your southern drawl is painful."

"Whatever, like your British accent is believable?"

"Her British accent is totally believable," Zeb said, sidling up to the bar as he got ready for the evening shift.

"It is not," Aidan said.

"Is too. Last week she had an entire conversation with an English table from Surrey and they asked what part of London she was from."

I threw a look at Aidan and said in a British accent, "*I'm very posh*. Okay, guys, have a good rest of your night, I'm off."

"To do what?" Zeb asked.

"I have absolutely no idea," I said. "I might bake cookies." More like I'd try to sit down and write. I was actually looking forward to it. The parody of a romance novel was slowly coming together.

"You're wild," Zeb said.

"Don't I know it." With a wave, I headed out. I looped my scarf around my neck, bundling up for the angry March weather. Winter just kept looming. I wasn't paying attention to where I was going and almost bumped into someone. "Sorry," I muttered.

"Sibby?"

"Yes?" I didn't recognize the man in front of me.

"I'm Taylor."

"Sorry, I'm drawing a blank."

"Matt's Taylor," he clarified.

"Oh, *that* Taylor." I tried to move around him, but he gently put up a hand to stop me.

"Listen, I don't mean to make you uncomfortable—"

I barked out a laugh. "A little late for that, don't you think? What are you doing here? Were you waiting for me?"

"Yeah, sorry, I'm not trying to go all single-white-male on you. I just wanted to talk to you."

"Why?"

"Because you won't talk to Matt, and he's pretty torn up about it."

"Why?" I adjusted my stance, becoming pugnacious.

"Really? He cares about you."

"Then maybe he shouldn't have...done what he did."

"I agree."

"You do?"

"Well, yeah. But, sometimes on our quest to find ourselves, other people get hurt in the process. I wish it wasn't the case, but it's the truth."

"You're a yogi, aren't you? You're all Zen and shit."

"I'm not Zen," he promised. "I just know what it's like to hide who you really are, to feel like you can't tell people for fear of judgment."

"Are you saying this is my fault? That I'm to blame for Matt keeping his sexuality hidden for so long?"

"No, I'm not——"

"Do you know how many trust issues I have now? I might have to see a shrink to reconcile all this crap!" I shook my head. "I've got to go. Tell Matt... You know what, I don't care what you tell him, just leave me the hell alone. The both of you!"

"Aren't you worried?" Annie asked over dinner the next

night. We were at our favorite Thai place in Union Square, equidistant from both our neighborhoods.

"About Taylor?" I shook my head. "Should I be?"

"He waited outside of work for you, which is kind of scary."

"I guess. He wasn't fearsome. Fierce, yes, fearsome, no."

"What he said to you…"

"Yeah?"

"It was kind of valid, wasn't it? Like, he kind of had a point."

"You think I should talk to Traitor—I mean, Matt?"

She sighed. "He emailed me."

I raised my eyebrows. "Wow, this week keeps getting weirder and weirder. What did he say?"

"Just asking after you, wondering why you still haven't contacted him for a coffee-date."

I grunted in response.

"I didn't reply to him. Sent it to junk mail."

"Thanks."

"He lost me in the break up. Not that he ever really had me."

"We're a package deal, aren't we?" I teased.

"Yes, we are. Caleb has pointed that out. He said I need to pay more attention to him. Like sex isn't enough?"

"Men." I shook my head.

"Right? It's like he wants to talk about stuff and I'm like, really, do we have to?"

"He writes you poetry, doesn't he?" I joked.

She didn't reply.

"Oh my God, he totally does!"

"You *cannot* tell anyone that," Annie hissed. "Not even Aidan. *Especially* not Aidan."

I grinned. "So, is it any good?"

Annie blushed. "What do I know about poetry?"

"It is! He's a good poet!"

"Shut up."

"You're happy."

"Maybe. I removed the Tinder app from my phone…"

"*Whoa*. Hold on. *Whoa*."

"I know."

"Hey, Annie?"

"Yeah?"

"It's okay not to answer when I call, you know. It's not your job to take care of me."

She smiled. "Well, damn. Maybe I need a new hobby?"

Natalie and I met for coffee before work. I hadn't seen her for a few days, but she looked at peace. Happy, even.

"I told Tad," she said, stirring her chamomile tea.

"And?" I demanded.

"He was really good about it. Like, so good—and calm. He was as calm as I was freaking out." She smiled.

"So what's going to happen?"

"We're going to move in together and take it from there."

"I think that's very wise," I said with a grin. "When are you going to tell people at work?"

"When I have an obvious baby bump. Maybe not even then."

"You'll tell Zeb though, right?"

"Yeah, I'll tell him. Surprisingly, he can totally keep a secret."

"Break the news to your parents yet?"

"Nope. And don't guilt trip me over that, okay?"

"No guilt here. I didn't tell my parents for four months that I got fired and cheated on. I'm not in the position of giving advice."

She smiled. "Let's talk about you. What's new with you?"

"Uhm, the guy Matt cheated on me with accosted me outside of Antonio's."

"Are you making shit up just to make me feel better?"

"I wish."

She laughed. "You're better than reality TV."

"What's this?" the guy asked.

"The duck breast," I answered.

"I didn't order this."

"Yes, you did."

"No, I ordered the duck pasta."

"No, you ordered the duck breast," I insisted.

"No, I really ordered the duck pasta."

"Remember when I repeated back your order and asked how you wanted the duck breast cooked? You said medium. Why would I take a temperature on a pasta?"

"I don't know."

"Exactly."

We stared at each other and finally the guy said, "The duck breast looks really good." He picked up his fork and knife and I breathed a small sigh of relief. You couldn't have paid me enough to go back into the kitchen at that moment. Julian was having a meltdown about the risotto he'd added to the night's specials. Everything had to be timed perfectly in a restaurant to get food out to people hot and fresh. Risotto took thirty minutes to cook and threw off the entire line. Why he decided to do this, I'd never know.

"He's going to give himself a heart attack," I said to Zeb when we heard Julian yelling in French.

Zeb snorted. "Don't tease."

"You guys ready to order?" I asked a table of four men. They were drinking a bottle of our most expensive Barolo, so I wanted to be attentive without too much suck-uppery.

"We'll start with a few appetizers," the ringleader said.

"Sure thing."

"Give us an order of *brajoot* and *mutzzarel*. We'll take an order of the fried *galamat* and some *scarole* with garlic and olive oil." He set his menu aside. "Can we order dinner later?"

"Yep. Whatever you want."

Even with my limited time at Antonio's, I already knew how to translate bastardized Italian. What did they really want to order? Prosciutto and mozzarella, fried calamari, and escarole with garlic and olive oil.

Like, so obvious. Duh.

After putting in their appetizer order, I headed to the coffee station and started prepping a six-cappuccino order. "Uh, Sibby?" Natalie said from somewhere behind me.

"You can work around me," I said.

"Oh, yeah, well no. I don't need to make coffee. Are you aware that there's a hole in your pants?"

"Hole?" I said distractedly, starting to steam milk with one hand while running the other down the back of my pants, searching for the rip. "Is it obvious?"

"Kind of. Your underwear is showing."

"What?" I hissed, turning off the steam wand and trying to get a good look at my rear end.

"Batman undies? Really?" Nat shook her head.

I groaned. That meant it was a really big hole.

"How did it happen?" she asked.

"I got stuck on one of the metal chairs in the courtyard earlier. I think it happened then." I pressed a hand to my eyes. "Just when I think my life is turning around, shit like this happens."

"Whatever, you could be the pregnant one," she said.

Chapter 20

Montepulciano d'Abruzzo [Mon-teh-pull-chee-ah-noh
dah-brut-zoh]:
1. Italian red wine, medium-bodied. Easy to drink.
2. The Budweiser of Italian wine.

I crumbed the table and put down dessert menus in
front of four middle-aged men. I reached for the olive oil
shaker as one of the men stated, "I'll have a cappuccino,
please."

"Sure, anyone else want coffee?" I asked. "Or an after-
dinner drink?"

"What's Amaro?" one guy asked.

"An herbal, rooty-like digestif. They taste like Italian cough syrup."

"Uhm, maybe we'll just have four Limoncellos," the guy who ordered the cappuccino said.

"Good choice. It's homemade."

I dropped off the Limoncellos and cappuccino when the spokesman of the group asked, "What do you do in your spare time? When you're not here."

"I'm a writer," I said honestly.

"Ah, what do you write?" he inquired.

"Oh, uhm, I'm writing a romance novel."

The man's eyes gleamed.

Stupid, Sibby. Really stupid.

"Romance novel, huh?" he pressed.

"Yeah."

"Well, if you need any help researching romance scenes, I'm available."

His friends guffawed like the aging frat boys they were.

"Ew," I blurted out. "I mean…Nope, *ew* was the right response."

The men stopped laughing and stared at me in stupid confusion. I gathered up the dessert menus and said, "I'll bring the check."

"But—"

"And I won't tell my manager you sexually harassed me."

Fifteen minutes later, the men were gone. "They leave an okay tip?"

I looked at the older woman sitting at a table for two, but she was by herself. I smiled. "Thirty percent. Think I shamed them into it."

She laughed. "I like that you didn't let them get away with it."

"I'm a server, not a servant. Some people think they

can say and do anything because I bring them food and alcohol."

"Is it true? What you told them? Are you really writing a romance novel?"

"Yeah, I am. Though it's kinda coming out funny and not sexy."

The woman looked at me for a long moment and said, "I'm a literary agent." She reached in her purse and grabbed a business card, handing it to me. "When your book is written, I'd love to read it."

I blinked. "Thank you." I held out my hand to introduce myself. "I'm Sibby."

"Alex. Seriously. I want to read your book when you're done." She gathered her belongings, scooted out of the booth, and left the restaurant. I stared after her, wondering if all the crap I had been through in the past few months, and all the detours in my life, had brought me to this moment—this chance meeting with a literary agent. Nothing might come of it, but I gripped the business card for all it was worth.

"Is it just me, or is there a new level of stupidity tonight?" Zeb asked. "I had one table ask me for a *chee-an-tee* and a *rice-ling*."

"Good God. I had a customer ask me if beefsteak tomato was a type of beef," I said.

"People sat themselves. How hard is it to wait? They make you wait at Olive Garden! And we're better than Olive Garden."

"Yeah, we're much more like Macaroni Grill," I quipped.

Zeb shook his head, diamond studs winking in the dim light. "I have never been so glad to be done."

"You say that every night you work. You know that right?"

"Yeah, and your point?"

"Seek help," I teased.

"You want to go grab a drink?"

"I would, but I'm meeting my best friend."

"Is that why you're in such a good mood?" he demanded.

"I'm not in that good of a mood."

"Yes, you are. Is it—" He gestured with his chin in the general direction of Aidan who was talking to a regular guest at the end of the bar, the guy we called "Mr. Saturday Night". Mr. Saturday Night came in all the time, dressed in 1950s garb, thinking he was cool, thinking he was a high roller.

He was creeptastic.

I had a low creeper tolerance, and after he asked if I had a boyfriend, I refused to wait on him. Zeb had no problem waiting on Mr. Saturday Night, hitting on him to give him a dose of his own medicine.

It was awesome to watch.

"He's part of it. But, I don't know," I admitted. "I just have this overall feeling of goodness. Like things have finally turned around for me." I was still riding high from the agent's business card I'd gotten the other night.

"And customers tonight didn't ruin that for you? Wow, you must be at peace with stuff."

A table of two men from my section stood up and put on their coats, laughing and joking. They passed by the bar where Zeb and I were standing, doing our checkouts.

The dark-haired Wall Street looking guy said to me, "Thank you so much for everything."

"My pleasure. Have a good night."

"Are you gonna do it," the blond guy asked.

Wall Street shot his friend a look, reached into his coat pocket, pulled out a business card, and handed it to me. "I'd like to take you out sometime. Call me."

I took his business card and stuttered, "Uhm, yeah, okay, thanks." My week for business cards, apparently. Wall Street gave me a pearly white smile. He turned back to his friend and they left, leaving me stunned.

What the hell was going on with me? Did I scream sex or something? My server uniform was boxy and unflattering, and if they got too close to me, they'd smell *Eau d'fryer*. And I'd bought new pants, so there was no way they'd seen the Superman underwear I was sporting.

I must've won him over with my personality.

Weird.

"I think Aidan's head is about to explode," Zeb said.

"Huh?"

"Look at him. Damn, he's got that sexy, jealous, broody thing going on. Guess he doesn't like people trying to take you away from him."

"Shut up, Zeb."

"What? No one can hear us. Besides, he's the one who's no longer acting like a manager. Jealous, broody boyfriend, party of one!"

I refused to look at Aidan. "And that's my cue," I said. "Exit stage right."

The bar was dark and the floor was littered with peanut shells. Annie and I were already drunk, having done a few rounds of shots the moment we entered the door.

"Oh my God, answer your phone!" Annie demanded.

"No! Aidan knows I'm out with you."

"But you snuck out of there," she said. "For all he knows, you're calling the guy who gave you his card."

"I threw it in the trash! And if he's thinking that I'm calling some other guy, then he doesn't know me. Besides I gave him a key."

"You gave him a key?" she asked. "How did I not know about this?"

"I don't know. Didn't I tell you?"

"Uhm. No."

"Sorry." I tapped my head. "I have a lot of stuff going on up here."

"You're dating in secret."

"So?"

"So, all the rules are different when you date someone in secret." I looked at her through bleary eyes, not understanding. "He's insecure, you idiot."

"You're telling me that Aidan—hot, wonderful, adorable Aidan—is insecure?"

"I'm gonna let you in on something—guys get insecure. And not just in bed."

I rested my face on the scarred wood bar and groaned.

"I wouldn't put your face there," Annie commented. "You don't know what's been on it."

I lifted my head immediately. "I can't talk to him like this."

"Like what?"

"Drunk."

"Weren't you hammered the first couple of times you guys hung out?"

"I've evolved."

"Liar Pants."

I sighed when my phone started dancing across the bar again. Before I could decide if I wanted to answer it or not, the big, tattooed bartender picked up my phone and said, "Hot girl's phone, how may I help you?"

"Dex!" Annie hissed.

I lunged for Dex, but he easily evaded me, and I slid across the bar top, nearly falling into a sink of ice on the other side.

"Sibby!" Annie cried. "What are you doing?"

"Agh!" I would've fallen onto the floor, but Dex easily wrapped an arm around me and hoisted me up.

"Dude, relax," Dex said into my phone. "Here she is." He gave me my cell and I glared at him. "Need a leg up back to your seat?"

"Bite me."

"Don't tempt Dex," Annie warned.

"Too late." Dex lifted my free arm and gnawed at my bicep through my sweater like a cartoon character.

"Sibby!" Aidan yelled from behind me, standing in the doorway of the bar.

I looked at him, then at my phone, then at Dex, who was still biting my arm. "What are you—we're on the phone!"

"We are," he said to me and then switched his gaze to Dex. "You gonna let go of my girlfriend's arm?" He looked ready to attack.

"Maybe," Dex taunted.

"Aidan, seriously, what are you doing here?" I demanded.

"I texted him where we were," Annie said. "I was tired of you complaining."

"This is not what this looks like," I said immediately, trying to shake Dex off.

"It looks like you've got a very big, very tatted bartender biting your arm."

"Oh," I said, striving for clarity through my drunken haze. "Then it's exactly what it looks like."

"I've known Dex for years. He's harmless," Annie insisted. "Well, most of the time."

"Seriously, I'm giving you three seconds to let go of my girlfriend before I leap over the bar."

Dex smirked and dropped my arm. "She's all yours. Too scrawny for me anyway."

I looked at him. "Who you calling scrawny?"

"Sibby, don't push your luck," Annie warned.

"Can we talk outside?" Aidan asked me.

"It's cold outside."

"Can we talk in the back corner?" Aidan relented.

I nodded and scooted out from behind the bar. Aidan followed me and I didn't even try and stop the babbling that was ensuing. "Listen, before you say anything, I threw that guy's card away."

"Okay," Aidan said, taking my hand and making me sit next to him.

"And that crap with Dex? I have no idea. He just picked up my phone and made a bad situation worse."

"Okay."

"Will you stop saying okay? You're not okay. I saw how you looked when that guy gave me his business card, but I had no intention of using it. Honest."

He peered at me curiously. "I know that."

"Then what was with the gritted jaw and jealousy?"

"God, you're obtuse."

"That's a really good word," I said. "Very SAT prep."

"You're ridiculous," he said, a small smile forming on his lips.

"Finally! A smile!"

As quick as the smile came, it disappeared. "I can't keep doing this."

"Doing what?" I demanded. "Getting jealous and me getting drunk? I agree. It's bad form. I think I'm becoming an alcoholic."

He shook his head. "You're not an alcoholic."

"Okay, what are you talking about then?"

"I hate this dating in secret crap. I'm an adult. I want to be able to kiss you in public, hold your hand in public—"

"You're not talking public, you're talking about everyone at Antonio's knowing."

"So what?" he yelled, finally getting mad. I'd never seen him mad. It was weird. So anti-Aidan. "We're not in high school and I'm done sneaking around."

"There are two of us in this situation—"

"Relationship," he clarified. "We're in a relationship."

"Fine. Relationship," I relented. "I don't want it broadcasted all around the restaurant! I'm trying to get rid of the drama in my life, not add to it!"

We glared at each other.

"I quit," I said.

His face went slack, the anger draining from him. "What?"

"Yeah, consider this my two weeks' notice. I'm done."

"But you can't—not because of this—"

"Try me," I dared. "I don't like being backed into a corner. And if you want us to be out in public together, then fine!"

"You can't quit! Natalie just quit!"

My head spun with anger, alcohol, and the change in conversation. "What?"

"She talked to Jess after her shift. You can't quit and leave us in a lurch!"

"Well, you can't have it all the ways you want it!" I yelled. I took a step back from him. "I need to get out of here."

"I'll go with you."

"No, I need time away from…all this." I looked at him and shook my head. "I'm right back where I started. Knee deep in drama and confusion."

"Sibby—"

"Please, Aidan, just give me some time, okay?"

I headed home, wondering what I was going to do. I pulled out my phone, scrolling through my email. There was already a note from Natalie telling us that she was leaving and that she had enjoyed her time at Antonio's.

I hit reply to her email and asked if she had told Jess she was pregnant, and that I was thinking about quitting because Aidan wanted to go public with our relationship. I hit send, and the email went through right before I lost service.

The train creepy-crawled all the way to Bedford Avenue and I almost fell asleep. At last, the train stopped, and I got out from underground. The sidewalks were slick with salt and melting snow and it was cold. My phone chimed. My hands fumbled to unlock it and it slipped from my grasp, clattering to the ground.

"Doh!" I scooped up my phone—the screen was cracked and dark and when I tried to turn the phone on, it remained stubbornly shut off. Just another thing I'd have to deal with tomorrow.

Joy.

The bus wasn't coming any time soon, so I grabbed a cab that cost me eight bucks. I got home and hung up my coat, wondering why my apartment felt so empty.

Aidan not being there felt weird. Really weird. And sad. Like I'd gotten a terrible haircut and couldn't look at myself in the mirror. Or something way less shallow.

No. Aidan was a rebound. I was projecting feelings on him. Right? But then why did I give him a key?

"Ah, crap," I muttered.

I was in love.

I made myself some soup while I read through the day's Tweets on my laptop, trying to ignore my feelings for Aidan. I wrote *Tragedy + Time = Comedy #lifetheme* before shutting off my computer and passing out on the couch.

I woke up with a hangover and reached for my phone before remembering it was still broken. Grumbling, I climbed off the couch and trudged to make coffee. I slurped some down, popped a few Aspirin, and got dressed. The Verizon store was only a few blocks from my apartment.

"I need a new phone," I told the young guy behind the counter, handing over my damaged phone.

"Do you have phone insurance?" he asked.

"Probably. I'm a *klutz*," I explained, giving him my personal info so he could pull up my account.

He smiled. "Yeah, you have insurance. That will get you a replacement phone. Same one you've got."

"Let's do it."

"Unfortunately, I don't have any in the store at the moment. I can get one in a few days, or you can head to the Union Square location and get a new one today."

I made a face. I didn't have to work for two days. The last thing I wanted to do was go into Manhattan on my day off. "I'll just wait. Thanks."

Maybe it would be good to be unplugged for a little while. I could try yoga or meditation, get back in touch with… Who was I kidding? I'd go crazy without my phone for a few days.

When I got home, I logged onto Facebook, frowning when I saw seventeen notifications. I started reading the messages; they were all from co-workers wondering how long I'd been with Aidan.

Confused and dumfounded, I wondered how the hell they knew what I had tried to keep a secret for so long. Zeb and Natalie had kept quiet. I thought back to the previous night and my heart began to pound. I opened my email and went to my sent folder. I clicked open the email I'd sent to Natalie…

And the entire staff.

Oops.

Chapter 21

Zeppole [zeh-poh-lee]:

1. Deep fried dough fritters, usually topped with powdered sugar.

2. Meh.

I wasted no time sending an email, Facebook message, wall post, et cetera to Annie, demanding that she come over as soon as possible. She arrived forty-five minutes later, holding a bag filled with wine bottles, as if she already knew all the drama that had gone down. Then again, she was dating Aidan's best friend.

"Hi, my name is Sibby. I'm clumsy and I make really

bad decisions," I said to Annie, holding out my hand as though we had just met.

Annie nodded. "Yeah, I know, I'm there for most of them."

I slapped my forehead. "I dropped my phone, it shattered, and then my life shattered. How's that for irony?"

"Have you been drinking?"

"No, as of now, I'm totally dry. Bad stuff happens when I drink."

"Tell me what happened after you left the bar."

So I did.

She shook her head and smiled.

"I know! This is a new level of crazy—even for me."

"And you haven't been in communication with Aidan or the restaurant since all this went down?"

I shook my head. "My phone is still broken. I don't get a new one for a few days."

"And Aidan didn't come over here demanding to talk to you?"

I shook my head again. "Have you seen him?" Annie hesitated, and I verbally jumped all over her. "What, what is it?"

"Aidan quit."

"What?" I yelled. "He did what?"

"Caleb told me he quit," she explained.

"But, why?"

"Because he doesn't want *you* to quit Antonio's, and he doesn't want you to break up with him."

"Huh?"

"This is the grand gesture," she explained slowly. "I thought you read romance novels?"

"I do."

"I thought you watched rom-coms?"

"Yeah, I do, okay? But it's not like any of that is real life."

"You've got to do something."

"Like what?" I demanded.

"Aidan is not Matt."

"I know that."

"Do you? Aidan quit his job instead of losing you."

"What an idiot," I muttered softly, my insides going all gooey and girly.

"You *lurve* him, don't you?"

"Pulling out the *lurve* card, huh?" I asked.

Lurve was a word Annie and I had heard in college and decided to use when we were drunk and mushy over the college boyfriends we'd given our virginities to. Naively, we thought we'd be with them forever, so we'd coined the term "lurve of your life", which was so much greater than regular love. The boys hadn't stuck, but the phrase did.

"Aidan's done everything you wanted to do. And what have you given him besides cookies and sex?"

"I gave him a clothes drawer. And a key."

"Whoop-dee-fricken-do."

"I did just get out of a relationship."

"That was months ago, and besides it was a dead relationship where you were nothing more than a cover for a closeted gay guy. Which is totally his issue, by the way, not yours."

"Tell that to my ego."

"We're not talking about your ego, we're talking about your heart."

"Whoa there—you sound like a rom-com BFF."

"Well, it is my job to talk sense into you. Let's say Matt wasn't gay and you guys stayed together. Your relationship would've been like eating a dry turkey sandwich for every meal for the rest of your life. *Forever.*"

"What does that even mean?" I demanded.

"It means he had no flavor, and eventually, you would've become that way, too."

"I can't do this now."

"Oh, we're doing this," she stated.

"You're drunk," I accused.

"Good of you to notice."

"When did that happen?"

"There's a flask in my purse. It's empty."

"I needed you clear-headed!"

"And I needed to get drunk!"

"Why?"

"Because Caleb asked me to move in with him."

"What!" I yelled.

"I know!" she yelled back.

"This is unbelievable."

She nodded. "I said yes."

"Should we toast?"

"What are we toasting?" Annie asked.

"To Hell freezing over. You found a guy you want to live with. I never thought that would happen."

"That makes two of us."

We talked for hours and then fell asleep in my bed. I woke up spooning her. I gently disengaged from my best friend, dashed off a quick note, and left. I headed to Peter

Pan, grabbed a couple of breakfast sandwiches and donuts and tried not to think about my breakfast date with Aidan when I'd taken him to the bakery.

Gah! Stupid boy!

What was he thinking, quitting? I still didn't know the damage I'd actually caused by my dramatic, drunken email to the entire staff, but I didn't expect it to be at all good. Even though Aidan had quit, I doubted I still had a job. The least I could do was call Jess and face the wrath. My adult-o-meter sprang up, telling me it was the right thing to do.

I got back to the apartment just as Annie was setting up the coffee maker. "Breakfast," I said, holding up the bakery bag.

"Good. I feel like crap on rye," she admitted.

"Do you think, maybe we should join a gym instead of drinking?"

She looked at me for a full three seconds before we both said, "Nahhhh."

"So you and Caleb—moving in together," I said, unwrapping my bacon, egg, and cheese on a toasted poppy seed bagel.

"Yeah, I know. I wonder what my parents will say."

"Your dad will ask if he's a Red Sox fan."

Annie grinned. "Which he is, thank God."

"And your Mom will be overjoyed, considering she thinks you're too emotionally stunted to ever settle down. You're broken."

"Settle down? Whoa, whoa, whoa. Let's not go that far."

"If you start telling me you guys are going to throw dinner parties and stuff, I'm divorcing you," I stated.

"That's fair. And if I decide I ever want to throw a dinner party, please smack me."

"On my honor as your best friend."

We were halfway done with our egg sandwiches when she asked, "What are you going to do about work—and by work, I mean Aidan."

"I have no idea," I said truthfully. The more I tried to think about it, the more confused I became. "As for work, I'm dreading opening my email. Jess has a habit of yelling in all caps. It's scary."

"Tell you what," Annie said, wiping her hands. "I'll go through your emails for you. Screen them."

"Really? That would be kind of amazing." I got up to get my laptop and brought it to her. She opened it and began scrolling. "Any word from Aidan?"

She shook her head. "Do you want there to be?"

"I don't know. I'm too hungover to think straight."

"There's a message from Jess."

"Is it bad? Is it mean? Should I cry?"

"Calm yourself," Annie said. "She wants to know if you'd come in a few minutes before your next shift."

"So she can fire me in person?"

"You really think she's going to fire you?"

"Wouldn't she?"

"Doubt it, she probably just wants to make sure you're not filing a sexual harassment case."

"And how would that sound? Nice, hot guy, who wears plaid and takes care of me wants to date and maybe get a puppy. I need to get out of here," I said. "I can't sit around in this apartment and think about the different piles of crap that have become my life."

"You need to get a new phone."

"I am getting a new phone. It will just take a few days. Besides, if there is any time to untether myself, it's now. I'm under the radar. I'm staying away from technology."

I was running late. Later than late. I'd gotten my new phone from the Verizon store, but hadn't had a chance to set it up, and then had to book it to the train. There was no way I was going to be early for my shift—I'd be lucky if I was on time.

Maybe it was better that way, so I didn't have to have a sit-down with Jess. I'd get onto the floor, slap a smile on my face, and figure everything else out later.

I was ten minutes late for my closing shift and already the bar and hostess areas were flooded with customers. I squeezed through the throng and made my way downstairs. I changed in record time and was back upstairs looking for Jess. She was at the hostess stand and looked like she was already harassed and annoyed.

She was probably missing Aidan's helpful presence. I swallowed. "Jess," I called.

Jess turned around and breathed a sigh of relief. "Good, you're here."

"Sorry I'm late. Train traffic."

She nodded absently. "Listen, you have a guest tonight who is proposing to his girlfriend. They requested the courtyard. His friend is going to film the entire thing. They're coming in at 7:00 p.m."

"Prime time, excellent."

"Specials are the same. We'll talk later, okay?"

I nodded.

"Don't worry, it's going to be fine," she whispered.

I let out a breath I hadn't known I was holding. I walked into the dining room, ready to face my co-workers and customers.

"You're alive!" Zeb greeted.

"Barely."

"You went underground."

"Completely. Phone broke and I avoided social media."

"Is it all still a mess?"

I nodded.

There was no more time to talk considering we were about to be knee deep in the rush. An hour later, Mr. Proposal sat in my section. His friend was with him and they set the table with a huge vase of roses. The girl wasn't going to be very surprised, unless she was an idiot.

"Can we have a bottle of champagne chilling on ice please? After I propose, will you just open it and bring it over?" he asked me. "My friend will give you the signal."

The friend shook my hand and then fiddled with his camera. Mr. Proposal pulled out his phone and said in nervous excitement, "She's here!"

A few minutes later, a beautiful, tall, thin woman—obviously one of New York's prettiest people—sauntered into the courtyard, waving at her boyfriend who was about to become her fiancé. She kissed him on the lips, and he held out her chair for her. The friend with the camera was on the other side of the courtyard, filming from the moment the couple sat down. I discreetly hung out in the opposite corner, waiting by the ice bucket for the signal to bring over the champagne.

"Oh my God, yes!" I heard the girl shriek.

The friend didn't need to tell me anything since I'd heard the woman shout out her acceptance. I was reaching for the bottle of champagne when Aidan rushed into the courtyard, barreling towards me.

"What are you doing here?" I demanded in surprise.

I struggled with the champagne bottle's foil wrapper.

Caleb trailed behind Aidan and said, "I'm sorry, Sib, we were out drinking and he wanted to come here, and I couldn't stop him."

"I miss you," Aidan blurted out. He was standing so close to me that I could smell the liquor on his breath. Aidan was a tall guy, so for him to be glassy-eyed and honest meant he'd had a good amount to drink.

"Ma'am!" Mr. Proposal called. "May we have our champagne now?"

"Coming!" I said. The foil was finally off and I was unwinding the cage, careful to keep my thumb over the cork.

"Sibby," Aidan bemoaned dramatically.

"Aidan, I can't do this right now," I pleaded. "Caleb, take him to my apartment, okay?"

"Keys?" Caleb asked.

"Aidan has a set."

"Dude, you've been withholding information from me," Caleb said. "Come on, buddy, you'll talk to her later."

"No!" Aidan said. "Now! I want to talk right now. I love you!"

"Ah, jeez dude," Caleb breathed, shaking his head.

My secret boyfriend had just told me he loved me, and I wanted to tell him I loved him, but I was a bit busy.

And the damn cork wouldn't come out of the damn bottle!

"Sibby?"

"What!" I snapped, looking towards a man as he strolled toward me in the courtyard. "Matt? What the—"

"Do you work here?" he asked.

I hadn't seen him since the night I broke my nose. Matt looked...

Gayer.

He was tanner, more muscular, and wearing a lavender shirt. There was a lot of product in his hair. Guess he'd really found himself in the months after we'd split up. Wish I could've said the same.

"Yeah, I work here. Nice shirt, Matt."

"I've been trying—"

"Ma'am, the champagne?" I heard in the background.

I ignored Mr. Proposal and said to Matt, "I know you've been trying to get ahold of me."

"What the hell are you doing here?" Aidan demanded, looking at Matt.

"You're the guy from—" Matt tried to ask.

"Yes. I'm the new boyfriend."

"Excuse me," Mr. Proposal said. "We're still waiting on our champagne. We are the ones celebrating our engagement here."

I gave him an apologetic look as I took a step closer to them. "Sir, I'm sorry, this cork is—"

Pop!

The cork burst out of the bottle. I watched it fly through the air in what seemed like slow motion, and cringed when it hit Matt in the eye. He covered his face and howled in agony while champagne spewed all over the newly engaged couple and me.

The courtyard was suddenly silent. Even Aidan, drunk as he was, stared at me with his mouth hanging open. Matt's cries had turned into a whimper. It was like everyone was waiting for me to say something.

I sighed. "That puts the *pain* in champagne, doesn't it?"

Chapter 22

Tortelloni [tort-eh-loh-nee]:
1. Half-moon shaped, stuffed pasta.
2. Just call it a freakin' ravioli, okay? Jeez.

The engaged couple got their meal for free, Matt went to the ER in an ambulance, and after Caleb carted Aidan out of Antonio's, I finally sat down with Jess in the office. I was back in my street clothes, my sticky, wet server uniform by my side in a plastic bag.

Jess looked tired. I made her tired. My drama made her tired. "You outed Natalie."

I winced. I hadn't talked to Nat and I needed to. But I'd been avoiding it.

Shocker.

"I told Aidan that you guys dating wasn't a problem."

"Then why did he quit?" I wondered.

She paused. "He has his reasons. I'm guessing you haven't talked to him since all that went down."

I shook my head. "Have you?"

"Aidan and I are friends outside this job. We used to work together years ago at a steak house. Our friendship comes first—and he didn't even tell *me* about you guys. That stings. It also shows me how much he cares about you if he's willing to keep secrets not just from me as his boss but also me as his friend."

I was quiet for a moment and said, "I quit. I'd rather quit than have you fire me. I do have some pride. Not a lot —not after tonight, but there it is."

"You don't have to quit, and I'm not firing you. You still have your job."

"Thanks, but I think I need a fresh start, ya know?"

"Are you sure? I know a lot has happened but—"

"I'm sure. I really appreciate it, though," I said, standing.

She hugged me and said, "Aidan is one of the good ones."

"And there's the silver lining in all of this, huh?"

Drained, I climbed the stairs to my apartment. I wasn't cut out for crazy, but lately my life had been a revolving carousel of it.

Aidan opened my door, reached for me, and pulled me into a hug. I just let him hold me, and it was nice. I was being comforted.

"You still drunk?" I demanded.

"No, coming down."

"Hard?"

"I'll be okay."

"Should we wait to talk?"

"No, I'm sober enough to talk."

"You didn't have to quit," I said. "I would've fessed up before I let you walk out of Antonio's. What are you going to do?"

"That email was just a good excuse for a change. I'd been at Antonio's for two years. I was getting bored. Actually, the only reason I lasted as long as I did is because you ended up working there."

"You're going to get bored with me."

"I don't think that's possible."

"I don't believe you," I said. "It won't always be like this, you know."

He frowned. "Like what?"

"I won't always be this dramatic or theatrical. My life is bound to calm down."

"Okay."

"Okay? If my life calms down, then you'll definitely find me boring."

"Sibby," he said on a sigh. "I don't know a lot about dating and stuff, but I do know that all the relationships I've had fizzled out right around the three-month mark. The sex gets stale and there's nothing left to talk about, so I bail. But with you, that hasn't happened. There's nothing stale about you."

"I'm not a loaf of bread," I shot out. "Besides, we've been dating in secret. That makes things more interesting. How do you feel now that you can take me out in public and hold my hand and all that gooey relationship crap?"

"I'm excited for that gooey relationship crap," he admitted. "I like trying new things. I want to try new things—with you. Believe me, or don't. But through all this mess, I wasn't the one who decided I needed space or tried to hide our relationship. That was all you."

I bit my lip and looked away. He was right. I was still recovering from Matt's burn.

"I'm not going to do what Matt did to you," he said as if he could read my thoughts.

"What? You mean use me as a beard?"

He didn't laugh. "I mean, I'm not ever going to give you a reason not to trust me. When I say something, I mean it."

"So the love thing. That was real?"

"That was real."

"You meant it?"

"I did. I *do*."

I sighed. "I love you, too."

He grinned. "Good."

"I don't have shit figured out," I said.

"Me neither."

"I quit Antonio's. I'm unemployed."

"That makes two of us."

"Our best friends are moving in together."

"I—what?" He looked shocked.

"Caleb hasn't told you yet? Oops."

"Well, good for them. I was getting sick of Caleb's dirty socks. Now it can be Annie's problem."

I grinned. "It's amazing what women will put up with for a good…spoon."

I woke up the next morning feeling fairly optimistic, despite the fact that I had no idea what I was going to do about the messes in my life. I needed a really big mop. Aidan was in bed next to me and I was glad. I chose to focus on that. I kissed him awake and he smiled at me with a sleepy grin.

"Wanna spoon?" I asked.

"Spoon spoon, or, ya know, *spork*."

"You think you're so clever," I said.

"Not as clever as you."

"I don't spork without brushing my teeth first," I said, trying to get out of bed.

"You think too much." Aidan reached for me and made me forget all about brushing my teeth.

After, we got up and made coffee. I rummaged through the refrigerator intent on making breakfast while Aidan got on his phone. A few minutes later he said, "Uhm, Sibby."

"Yeah, hun?" I asked, my head stuck in the fridge.

"You might want to check Facebook…"

"Why?" I asked as I set the bacon and eggs on the counter.

"Where's your computer?"

"On the coffee table."

Aidan got up and went to get my laptop. He came back into the kitchen, the laptop open to my Facebook page. I scrolled through my newsfeed, seeing the same video linked to YouTube and shared to people's Facebook pages over and over.

I hit play on one and turned up the sound.

"What is this?" I asked, but as soon as the words left my mouth, it all became clear. The video was of me pegging Matt in the face with a cork in the courtyard of Antonio's and spraying champagne everywhere. "Oh, no."

"Shit, that cork really nailed Matt. This is awesome," Aidan said.

I continued to stare in horrified silence even after the video went dark. Aidan clicked the YouTube link. "Holy shit. Thirty thousand people have already seen it. Look at the comments! Sibby! You're a viral sensation!"

Aidan called in reinforcements and Caleb and Annie arrived within the hour. They'd seen the video and Annie said, "You both saw it in person. It's not fair."

"I was drunk, if it makes you feel any better," Aidan said. "So I don't remember a lot."

"That does make me feel better, thank you." Annie looked at me. "Have you gotten on Facebook recently?"

I shook my head. Annie bit her lip, looking like she was

in debate over what to say. Caleb took her hand and squeezed it. "Might as well tell her."

"Last I checked, that video had over one hundred thousand views."

"Fuck," I moaned.

Aidan piped up. "Do we know if you permanently blinded Matt? Does he have to wear an eyepatch the rest of his life?"

"He could totally do gay pirate porn," Caleb said.

I glared at him and Annie laughed. "I think I now owe him that coffee sit down," I said, rubbing my third eye.

"Just stay off Facebook," Annie said. "And tell Matt to stay off Facebook, too. Though I'm sure he already knows better."

"Well, I guess the one good thing is that my parents are completely unaware of this situation."

"Sib?" Aidan asked.

"Yeah?"

"Your parents are calling you." He held out my phone to me.

I took it and sighed. "They're going to have to change it from Murphy's Law to Sibby's Law." Shaking my head, I pressed the answer button. "Hey, parental units. No... What video?"

"This is awkward," I said.

"Very," Matt agreed.

We were both wearing very large sunglasses. Me to hide my face, since it was currently all over Facebook and YouTube and I was in New York City after all, and Matt because he was wearing an eyepatch over an eye that was apparently healing quite nicely.

"I'm really sorry about the cork."

"I kind of think it's karma," he admitted with a wry smile.

I chuckled nervously.

"I'm sorry, too, Sibby. I didn't mean to hurt you. It just all got so…and I didn't know how to tell you and…anyway, I'm sorry."

I nodded and took a sip of coffee to cover the unexpected emotion in my throat. I never thought I'd need to hear those words, but I did.

"Are you happy?" he asked me.

I thought for a moment. Was I happy? I was unemployed and my life was in chaos, but I had Aidan and good friends, and I was okay. I was going to be okay.

"Yeah, I am. Are you?"

He nodded.

"Taylor seems like he really cares about you," I pressed.

He smiled shyly. "I care about him, too. So, we're okay?"

"Yeah, we are."

We parted ways and I felt lighter than I could've possibly imagined. It felt good to be finished with that chapter of my life. Matt and I might never be friends, but if we ran into each other on the street, we wouldn't have to do that awkward thing of pretending we didn't know each other. Besides, if Matt hadn't royally screwed me over, I never would've partied with Annie that night on the Upper East Side, and meeting Aidan might have turned out very different if I'd met him at the restaurant.

Everything for a reason and all that.

I finally got up the nerve to call Nat. "I'm a shit," I said in way of apology.

"Yeah, you are," she agreed. "But I forgive you."

"Because we're really friends outside of the restaurant?"

"That, and because your mess is way bigger than my mess."

Perspective. I loved that in a friend.

I joined Aidan at an Irish pub on the Upper East Side for drinks.

"I'm sorry, I'm not sure I recognize you in your civilian clothes," Aidan teased, kissing me on the cheek.

"I'm not sure I recognize you without the stench of restaurant all over you," I joked back.

"This is nice," he said. "Isn't it?"

I grinned. "Better than nice."

"Pool table is free," he said. "You up for a game? It is how all this started."

"You romantic you. Guard the table, I'll get us another

round." I headed to the bar and waited for the bartender to come to me.

"Oh my God," a girl next to me said.

I glanced at her. "What? Is there something in my teeth? Not again…"

"You're the waitress in that video!"

"Yeah…wait, no, that wasn't me."

"Really?" She almost fell off her stool. "You look *just* like her. I watched that video, like, a hundred times."

"Oh, yeah?"

"I swear you look just like her," she said, pulling out her phone. A moment later, she was shoving her phone in front of my face and I was forced to watch myself and pretend that I found it hilarious, when mostly I just found it embarrassing.

She stuffed her phone back into her pocket. "Hey, Jason! Doesn't this chick look like that waitress in the video we saw?"

Jason was beefy and his chin disappeared into his neck —like a face cankle. A fankle. He stood next to Drunken Girl and looked me over. "Yeah, you do. God, that girl is really funny. I wonder if she blinded that guy."

My grin tightened.

"Sibby, what's taking so long?" Aidan called out, coming towards me.

Fankle and Drunken Girl's mouths dropped open. "And you're the guy," Drunken Girl murmured.

"What guy?" Aidan demanded.

"The guy who professed his love to the waitress—from the video."

I dropped my head into my hands.

"Can I get your autograph?" Drunken Girl asked me.

I blinked. "Uh, sure." I reached for a bar napkin and

the absent bartender finally arrived. "May I borrow a pen, please?" I asked him. He handed it over and I scribbled on the napkin.

I passed Aidan the pen and napkin. "Give them your autograph or we'll never get to play pool."

Chapter 23

Guanciale [gwan-chal-ay]
   1. Pork cheek.
   2. Chewy and weird. Kinda creepy.

"You wanna watch some late-night TV?" Aidan asked.

I threw my keys onto the coffee table and shrugged out of my layers. "Sure." I headed to the bedroom, wanting to get into comfortable clothes. After the drunks had asked for our autographs, we'd played a game of pool, but my heart hadn't been in it.

Aidan flipped on the TV and I heard the voice of New York's most prominent late-night talk show host through the clapping of the audience. When the spectators died down, the host introduced his guest, but I wasn't paying attention as I was looking for my favorite threadbare T-shirt and leggings.

"Sibby? You might want to come out here."

"In a sec!"

"Now!" he called back.

Grumbling and halfway dressed, I came into the living room and saw who was on screen.

It was the famous actor I'd spilled wine on at Antonio's.

"So, I heard you had a bit of trouble on your last trip to New York," the host said.

Famous Actor smiled. "News travels fast."

"Why don't you tell them about what happened," the host said, gesturing to the audience.

"Well, I was in New York a few months ago and I ate at one of my favorite restaurants. It's a great Italian place that makes its own fresh pasta…"

"Oh no," I murmured, my heart getting ready to burst out of my chest.

"Shhhh!" Aidan said.

"Our waitress was this really cute girl with big black glasses, right? The night was going pretty great, the food was excellent, my date was really into her kale," he turned and smiled at the laughing audience, "and then our waitress spilled wine all over me. Ruined my favorite cashmere sweater." The famous actor was grinning, and it showed his good humor.

"So, stuff like that happens to you, too, huh? Even you are not exempt?"

"Guess not." He shrugged. "She was as nice as can be about it, and I can afford a new sweater."

"As it turns out," the host added, "I know the restaurant you went to. And it seems this waitress has made it her mission to put on shows."

The lights on the stage dimmed and the big screen behind the host and the famous actor lit up. There I was—larger than life—opening a bottle of champagne on national television, the cork flying across the room and hitting Matt in the eye.

"Let's watch that part again—in slow motion," the host said.

The audience went crazy with laughter.

"I haven't seen comedy like this since Lucille Ball," the host said with a laugh. "We did some scouting and we found out her name."

"No," I whispered. "No, no, no."

"Sibby Goldstein, if you're watching, thanks for the laughs."

"I have thirty missed calls," I stated the next morning.

Aidan took my cell phone and crammed it between the couch cushions. "Don't look at that."

"I have to."

"No, you don't. Call Annie on my phone."

I took a couch pillow and put it over my head. "You're not even trying to talk me out of how bad this is."

"Easier just to let you have your fit of drama. Very Lucille Ball of you."

"Shut up!" I'd had a hard time falling asleep, and when I finally did, all I saw were images in my mind of the famous actor and the host pointing at the video of me on the big screen and laughing.

I threw the pillow away from my face and it hit the floor with a soft thud. "Two drunk people recognized me from the video in a dark bar in Manhattan, *before* it went on national television. What's going to happen now?"

"I have no idea."

Aidan's phone started going crazy. We looked at each other. "It's Jess," he said. "Should I get it?"

"Oooo-kay?"

Aidan answered his phone and a moment later handed it to me. "Hello?"

"You have to take your job back," Jess said.

"Good morning to you too."

"I don't have time for greetings," she said. "I've been at the restaurant fielding calls for hours. Everyone wants to eat here and be served by you. They all think you're going to do something that's going to make them part of the next viral video."

"People are insane."

"I'm well aware. So, will you come back?"

"And be the comedic waitress? I don't think so. Thanks for the offer, though."

"But—"

"Jess, you know I like you, but I so can't deal with this right now. I have to go, I'm sorry." I hung up the phone and sat in silence.

"Wanna go for a run?" Aidan asked.

"Um, hello, I didn't get this pale by being into sports."

He shrugged. "Want to go away together?"

My eyes got really wide as I stared at him. "Seriously?"

He nodded. "Why not? We don't have jobs. I've got a bit of savings and it's cold. Let's go somewhere tropical."

"That doesn't sound very responsible," I said.

"Come on, Sib, let's go away. I'm sure there are last minute deals and stuff. Think about it. Tomorrow we can wake up, hear the ocean from our hotel room, and drink our breakfast."

"When you put it that way…"

"We'll go away and leave all this. It will at least get us away from people who might recognize you for a while."

"Sold."

"You look ridiculous," Aidan said as we sat at our airport gate, waiting for our plane departure.

I lowered the sunglasses minutely but refused to take off the big straw hat. "You're the one wearing a Puka shell necklace and board shorts. We're not in the Bahamas yet."

"Just trying to get us in the mood. You're just trying to hide. No one will even know who you are."

"Doubtful. I'm not that lucky." I sighed. I'd forwarded our flight itinerary and hotel info to my parents and Annie, just so a few people knew what was happening. Annie quickly replied, saying she was glad I was grabbing life by the balls. She was deep in nesting mode and I worried that by the time I got back, she might have morphed into a Manhattan housewife.

Aidan leaned over to kiss me and grinned.

"Why are you grinning?"

"Because I can finally tell you why Julian was in such a good mood for so long. I'm no longer under obligation to keep it a secret."

"Finally, something good coming from us both being unemployed. Tell me."

"He auditioned to be on a new cooking show for reality TV and he made it."

"Julian is going to be a reality TV star?"

"Yep."

"What cooking show is it?"

"I don't know what it's called, but apparently it's like Survivor meets Master Chef. He has to cook in the wild and camp. Use what's available."

"Like grubs and stuff? Is he going to cook insects?"

"Probably."

"Gross." I shook my head. "What if he gets eaten by a bear?"

"That would make for really good TV," he pointed out.

"We're so watching that shit."

He laughed and stood up. "I'll be right back."

"Where are you going?" I asked, but he didn't reply. I watched him head to the airline counter and start conversing with the overworked, underpaid, middle-aged-gate agent. Within seconds, Aidan had the woman smiling and they both looked over at me. Had Aidan pulled out a white, fluffy kitten and given it to her?

Aidan came back, holding two new tickets and handed them over. I glanced at them and then at him. "First class?"

He grinned smugly.

"How?"

"I told her that I was planning on proposing to you on our vacation and I wanted to start the trip off right."

If I'd been drinking something, I'd have spit it all over him. Instead, my mouth went dry and I felt light-headed.

"Sibby? Sibby, stay with me." Aidan put his hand to the back of my neck, or tried to, but the straw hat got in the way. He flapped it off my head and got really close to me. He went in and out of my vision. "Sibby, I was kidding. I just told her it was your birthday. Take a deep breath. That's it. Good. Another one."

"Jesus, Aidan," I said when I could finally draw air into my lungs.

"Your reaction to my fake proposal is less than stellar, gotta say. I'm a little offended."

"I'm going through a lot right now."

"As always."

Four hours later, we were standing in a beautiful white lobby filled with fragrant flowers. I started to sneeze and my eyes began to water. "Crap, I forgot my allergy medicine."

Aidan sighed like he was tired, but with a grin, he pulled a small bottle out of his board shorts.

"You make me want to sing you Usher songs," I said, taking the bottle from him.

"Pop one, then let's go down to the beach," he said.

"We've only got a few more minutes of daylight. I want to catch the sunset."

"What about our bags?" I asked.

"We'll have the bellman take them up to our room."

Hand-in-hand, we walked down to the surf. It was quiet and calm, and in the distance, I heard kids squealing with laughter, but aside from that and the waves, there was nothing. It was perfect. With my phone shut off and a thousand miles from New York, it was almost easy to imagine that there was nothing crazy going on in my life. I looked at Aidan. The guy I'd known for only seven months.

He glanced at me and smiled. "What are you thinking about?"

"You," I said, surprising us both.

"Good things or bad things?"

"Good. All good."

He gestured to the sand and we took a seat. The air was warm and smelled of the sea. I felt languid enough to become part of the ocean. Just let my bones slip into liquid and float away on waves.

"I really want to thank you," I said to him.

"For?"

I leaned my head on his shoulder. It was a nice shoulder. "For putting up with all the insanity. I don't know a lot of men who would stick around for this—even guys who were a few years in."

"Well, I wouldn't stick around for just anyone, you know? You're kinda special."

"Special as in that-girl-is-eating-her-hair special?"

He chuckled. "See what I mean? You make me laugh."

"Back at ya. Laughter is the best medicine. Unless you're really sick, then you should go to the hospital. Guess

I should thank you for that, too. Putting up with me through a broken nose."

"We've gone through a lot together, haven't we?" he asked.

I nodded. "We have, indeed." We were silent a moment and then I said, "If this were a romantic comedy this is the part where you'd propose."

"Jesus, Sibby, really?"

I lifted my head from his shoulder. "What?"

He rolled his eyes skyward, which I could barely see in the dying light. "Why you gotta beat me to the punch?"

"I was kidding!" I shrieked. Somewhere in the distance, a seagull cawed.

"Well, I'm not."

"Well, you should be," I stated. "You don't ask a girl to marry you when neither of you have jobs and no idea where your lives are going."

"That's *exactly* when you ask a girl to marry you! It's easy to propose when life is good. But what about when it's all going wrong, but you have so much fun together you don't care how much crap you have to sift through, you just want to work through it all with the person next to you." He looked at me. "What? No smart-ass retort?"

"I—" I didn't know what to say. When he put it that way, it made it hard to want to do the logical thing. Doing the logical thing hadn't been working out for me. It was boring and plain.

Logical was a dry turkey sub.

Had the last few months taught me nothing?

"We don't even live together!" I snapped.

"Then I'll move in," he snapped back.

"Fine!"

"Fine?"

"Yeah, fine to you moving in, fine to marrying you! You

happy? This is supposed to be romantic, you dink, and now we're fighting!"

"What do you want from me? I proposed on a beach."

I glared at him, and I was sure he was glaring at me, but I couldn't tell in the near dark.

"Are you turned on right now?" he demanded.

"Very."

"Want to go back to the room and have wild, crazy engagement sex?"

"Definitely!"

He stood up and then reached down to help me. He took me into his arms and leaned down to kiss me when something dropped on my shoulder.

"What was that?"

I felt Aidan chuckle against me. "I think a bird just pooped on you. But hey, it's supposed to be good luck."

Chapter 24

Fernet-Branca [fur-nay-brank-ah]:
    1. An Italian mint-flavored digestif.
    2. Tastes like toothpaste with alcohol. Pass.

After showering off my good luck, I got lucky. Very lucky. We ordered room service, which was totally frivolous, but I tried not to worry about it.

"I have some ideas about the future," Aidan said, when we were sitting outside on our private balcony. We were enjoying strawberries and a bottle of champagne under the stars. I had Aidan open the bottle—I didn't want to take any more risks with champagne corks.

"I thought you didn't care about that stuff."

"Do you really think I would've proposed if I didn't have an idea of what comes next?"

"I thought you were a *man without a plan* and that you were okay with that."

"I am okay with that. But you're not that kind of woman. You need security. I want to give you that."

"Even by changing who you are?"

He shrugged. "Gotta evolve. Separates us from the beasts, right?"

"I thought our opposable thumbs proved we were already evolved."

"Focus."

"Sorry. Go on."

"I really like the hospitality industry," he said.

"Why?"

He glared at me.

"Sorry, shutting up."

"As I said, I really like the hospitality industry, but I hate having a boss." He looked at me, and I nodded for him to continue. "Caleb and I have decided to open our own bar."

I blinked. "Really?"

He nodded. "We want to be partners. He likes bartending, so he's cool with being the front man. I'm good at managing, so it works. We found a place and have investors. It's right around Franklin and Calyer."

"You guys are opening a bar in Greenpoint?"

"That's the plan."

"Why not the Upper East Side?"

He shook his head. "I don't fit in there anymore, Sibby. I've bought one too many flannels."

I started to laugh. "Wow, you guys are really opening a bar."

He nodded. "What do you think?"

"I think we have a lot to celebrate," I said, jumping up from the chair and launching myself at him. I perched on his lap and kissed him soundly. "You asked me to marry you before you told me about the bar."

"Yeah."

"Wanted to see if I loved you for *you*, huh?"

He grinned. "Maybe."

I cupped his cheeks in my hands. "You done good. I'm proud of you. Does that sound condescending?"

"Yes."

I playfully punched him.

"But I know you didn't mean it that way, so it's all okay."

"Wow."

"What?"

"Sometimes life is *totally* a romantic comedy."

He shook his head. "Sibby. If that were the case, we would've met in a really cute way, like at a bookstore or a coffee shop—not at a bar on the night you got fired and you found your boyfriend cheating on you with a dude. And a bird wouldn't have crapped on you right after my proposal."

"Made our story special though, huh?"

"Special." He smiled. "Yeah."

"I didn't get you a ring yet," he said.

"That's okay." We were lazing by the resort pool under a canopy and I was sleepy with sun and piña coladas.

"I didn't want to give you something to throw at my head."

I laughed.

"Just kidding, I wanted you to pick it out yourself. You know, to be sure you actually like it."

"You could've asked Annie what I like."

"I didn't want her to slip up and tell you."

"Well done."

"Not all things are done by the seat of my pants," he said, pretending to be affronted.

"And what a nice seat it is." I sighed dreamily. "She totally would've spoiled it, too. Annie can't keep a secret. Not from me, anyway."

"Don't you want to call her and tell her the good news? Or what about your parents?"

"I'll call them from the airport on our way home," I said, my eyes closing. "I want to stay unplugged a little while longer."

"You're not scared of what they're going to say, are you?" he asked knowingly.

"I can hear it now: *Mazel tov*, Sib! Congrats on the engagement! So now what are you going to do? Have you sent out any resumes yet? What kind of job are you looking for? How much money do you have saved?"

Jewish guilt, it's a thing.

"That wasn't a very good impression of your mother."

I snorted. "It was supposed to be my father."

"Oh. In that case, the impersonation was uncanny."

"I need another drink," I said, sitting up.

"Ms. Goldstein?"

"Yes?" I asked, looking at the concierge who approached.

"You have a call," he said, handing me a phone.

"I have a call?" I asked.

"I tried to take a message for you, but the caller is most insistent on speaking with you."

"Who is it?" I asked, taking the phone.

When the concierge told me who was on the phone I didn't believe him, and from the look on Aidan's face, neither did he. I put the phone to my ear. "You are so *not* the funniest person in the world, Annie. I'm revoking your best friend title."

"Ms. Goldstein?"

I frowned in confusion. Either Annie was faking a deep, masculine voice really well or she'd gotten a voice box transplant.

"Ms. Goldstein?" the voice on the phone asked again.

"Yes," I croaked. "Here. Sorry."

"You're a hard woman to track down."

"Yeah, well, I'm on vacation," I said. "Who am I speaking to?"

He told me.

Holy. Shit.

"Is this some sort of prank?" I demanded.

"No, it's not."

"I don't believe you." I shot a look at Aidan, who was watching me in confusion.

"I had a feeling you wouldn't. Ask the concierge about your hotel room. Go ahead, I'll wait."

I looked at the concierge, but before I could say anything he said, "Your stay has been taken care of in full by the gentleman on the phone." As he finished his sentence, a waiter with a bottle of champagne came over and set the tray down next to us, filling our glasses and nodding before heading off.

I heard the voice on the phone say, "Yeah, you're welcome. Now listen I wanted to ask you something…"

"I'm going to throw up," I said. "I'm going to throw up on network television."

"You can do this," Aidan said, putting his hands on my shoulders. "Hey, hey, look at me, look at me."

I looked at him.

"You didn't sleep last night, did you?"

"No. I tried, but I just couldn't fall asleep. I feel like the walking dead, but I've had so much coffee I'm jittery."

"It's okay. Just pretend you're talking to a fifteen top. All you have to do is be your usual charming, witty self."

"I can't do that on command. What was I thinking? This is crazy."

"You were an actor in college," Aidan stage-whispered.

"Not a good one! Why do you think I became a writer?"

"So you could wear pajamas all day long?"

"It's like you know me," I said, momentarily distracted. "Is my dress okay? Do I stink of fear?"

"You're wearing my deodorant. Nothing is getting through that. You got this. Just smile and relax, and it will all be over soon."

"That's what they tell death-row inmates!"

"Hey, save the humor for the audience."

"You ready to go on?" a producer with a clipboard and a wireless headset asked. "We have to go now."

"Uhmmm, okay."

"Just look at the host. Talk to him, and pretend no one else is around. He'll get you through."

"Was this your idea?" I asked her.

She shook her head. "I wish. It's brilliant. Huge fan, by the way. That thing with the cork was amazing. Okay, go on out there." She gave me a little push, and with one last look in Aidan's direction, I walked out from behind the stage curtain into the studio.

The lights were bright, and as the audience clapped and yelled, I waved and then tripped on my way up the steps to the chair. I grinned widely, and then shrugged it off as the audience laughed. I shook the host's hand and he gestured to the guest chair. I took a seat and the audience calmed down.

"That was some entrance," he said with a smile.

"Sibby's Law," I explained. "I make Murphy look *goooood*. Stuff goes wrong around me."

The audience laughed and the host chuckled. "Thanks for being here tonight."

"You wouldn't take no for an answer," I quipped.

"It's true," the host said as he looked directly at the audience. "I tracked her down. She was in some tropical place." He pointed to my bare shoulders in my sleeveless dress. "You've got a little sunburn going on there."

"It's not a sunburn, it's a Jewish tan."

I felt my nerves unfurl as the audience roared with laughter.

"Aside from that trip up the stairs, you don't seem nervous. Are you nervous?"

"My fiancé talked me off a ledge right before I came on stage." I shot a look toward the direction of Aidan. "Oops. I don't think I was supposed announce that we're engaged. My parents are *so* going to kill me. Hi, Mom! Tell *Bubbe* I love her!" I waved to the cameras and the audience went wild.

I had four minutes left before I could slink off stage. Just enough time to spill water all over myself, get a run in my stocking while crossing my legs to cover the spill, and reach out more than once to play with the host's cheeks.

Bless his heart, he let me.

"They're like Play-Doh," I told the cheering audience as the host blushed and smiled.

My time on stage wrapped up and, with one last pinch of the host's cheek, I exited the stage. A producer ushered Aidan and me out the door towards a waiting limousine, and I started to think I could get used to this sort of treatment.

Jewish American Princess?

Check.

As the car pulled away and turned into traffic, Aidan put his arm around me. I snuggled up into him and sighed.

"Was I okay?" I asked.

"Okay? You were perfect."

"She's your mother," Aidan said with a grimace. "You have to talk to her." He thrust my cell phone at me.

"Hi, Mom," I said tiredly as I paced around the living room of my apartment. "I'm sorry you had to find out that way. No, I wasn't high on dope." I rolled my eyes. "No, I wasn't drunk. Seriously, I was just sleep-deprived and hopped up on caffeine to compensate. Well, I'm sorry, but you're just going to have to tell your Mahjong group that I don't deal well with the stage."

I held the phone away from my ear for a moment, put it back, and thrust it away from me again, and said to Aidan, "I can't keep anything to myself. Why did I have to go and announce our engagement on television?"

He grinned.

I shot him a look. "You're enjoying this, aren't you?"

"Just a little. Okay, a lot," he clarified.

"Mom…Mom…Mom, Mom! Stop! Yes, I'm engaged. Yes, to Aidan. Who else would it be? No, no, no, I'm not dating anyone else in secret. No, for the last time, I'm not pregnant! Mom, go eat your whitefish salad, I'll call you later, okay?"

I hung up and said to Aidan, "We just had a vacation. Why am I still exhausted? And if you say my life is exhausting, I'm gonna punch you."

"Wanna talk about something else?"

"Sure."

"I want to move my stuff in," Aidan said.

I nodded. "Should we do it tomorrow? We're having dinner with Caleb and Annie tonight."

"We are? Did I know about this?"

"No, of course not. You're the guy. You just show up when I tell you to show up."

"Is that going to be the theme of our life?"

"It already is," I teased.

"So what about the wedding? When is that going to happen?"

"I don't really want talk about the wedding, okay? Eloping is starting to become an appealing option."

"I'm down with that."

"Hah. My mother would never forgive me. She found out about our engagement on television, along with the rest of America. That's one strike against us and we're not even married yet."

He sighed. "So, you're going to let her decide everything, huh?"

"You ever try telling a Jewish mother she can't plan her daughter's wedding?"

"Uhm, no."

"Yeah, you don't. Just let her plan, and I'll show up when and where I'm told to show up."

"I thought that was my job."

"We have the same job," I explained. I had already mentally caved. I was not going to fight my mother on wedding details. I could see it now—goofy, poofy dress, too many flowers, and too many guests.

"Are we getting married under one of those tent thingies?"

"It's called a *chuppah*, and yes, I imagine so."

"Do I get to break a glass?" he asked, his eyes lighting with excitement.

"Totally. And when the wedding is over, you and I get to do the horizontal *hora*."

Epilogue

One Year Later

"Welcome back," the host said.

I settled into the guest chair and grinned. "Thanks for having me again."

"You were so much fun the last time, and besides, I need another cheek massage."

"I was a mess. You're a gentleman to pretend otherwise." I winked.

"The last time you were here, you were a recently unemployed waitress with a viral video, and now you're a *New York Times* best-selling author."

"Life's funny, huh?"

"So tell me how that happened? Usually when people go viral it's over pretty soon, but here you are."

"Yeah, I got kind of lucky. While I was waiting tables, I began writing a book. One night at the restaurant, I met a literary agent. She gave me her card and told me to contact her when I had a manuscript completed. She sounded genuinely interested in reading it. I thought, Nah, nothing will come from it."

"Guess you were wrong, huh?"

I grinned. "Very."

He reached for the book in front of him and held it up to the camera. "*Spanking the Spatula: An Erotic Comedy* by Sibby Goldstein."

"Have you read it?"

"I have."

"I wouldn't think it would be your cup of tea."

"What, are you kidding? Penis euphemisms galore. It's right up my alley." He pointed to the male cover model, whose chest was bare. "And look at those man nipples—"

"Mipples," I corrected.

Cue audience laughter.

The host laughed as well and continued, "Will you autograph it for me?"

He handed me a pen and I used his desk to dash off a quick note in the title page. I gave it back to him and he read out loud: Your cheeks are better than any model's mipples.

Everyone laughed.

"You should tell them what your book is about," he said.

"It's about a young woman who's going through the rigors of culinary school. She falls for one of her instructors and they like it dirty. You know, sauces and kitchen utensils kind of dirty. It's a comedy. My agent is calling the genre dirty chick-lit."

He set my book aside. "Rumor has it, you're also working on the next book in your erotic comedy series."

"The rumor is true."

"Do we have a title?"

I shook my head. "I was hoping you guys could help me with that?"

The host's brow furrowed in confusion. "Go on."

"I have three potential titles," I explained. "And I'd like the audience to vote for their favorite."

"You mean, you're going to let *them*"—the host pointed to the audience—"name your next book?"

"Yep."

"I love that idea!" he said with a huge smile. "Okay, tell us your titles."

"*Beating the Banana, Flicking the Fava,* or *Tickling the Turnip.*"

"Well, I definitely see a theme. Okay folks, pull out your phones and Tweet your favorite title to @sibbygold-stein. The title with the most Tweets will be the title of Sibby's next book." The host turned to me and changed the conversation, "Are you still engaged?"

I held up my hand to show off the gorgeous engagement ring Aidan and I had picked out in the diamond district.

Hello, kinda Jewish!

The audience cheered in excitement when I showed everyone the ring.

"I'm getting married this weekend."

"Are you nervous?"

"Yes, absolutely," I said with a straight face.

"You are?"

"Well, we're having a Jewish wedding. I'm afraid I'm

going to fall out of the chair. It would be just my luck, you know?"

He smiled. "I'll think good thoughts. So, what does your fiancé do?"

"He's a bar owner," I stated with pride. "He and his best friend opened a bar in Greenpoint a few months ago."

"What's the bar called? Maybe I'll stop by."

"Veritas."

"As in *in vino veritas?*"

"Exactly."

"Is it a cool place?"

"Very."

"Hipster bar?"

"I plead the fifth."

He laughed. "Listen, I have a surprise for you."

"A surprise for me?" I turned around in my seat, looking in the direction the host was pointing.

The famous actor I'd spilled wine on strolled out onto the sound stage. The audience's cheers were deafening.

"Oh my God," I said, standing so I could greet him.

Unfortunately, my feet tangled with one another and I tripped—right into the famous actor. He wasn't prepared for my assault and I knocked us to the ground, accidentally kneeing him in the *kishkes*. If that wasn't bad enough, I felt a sudden draft on my bum. Struggling to right myself, I looked back and saw that my skirt had flipped up. I was flashing the entire audience.

Thank God for superhero undies.

The famous actor was still moaning in pain underneath me as I struggled to lift myself off of him. I gave him my most sincere and apologetic look when I said, "I'm such a huge fan."

Sibby's Law.

It's a thing.

A Quick Guide To Yiddish

Bubbe: Grandmother.

Chuppah: Canopy that a Jewish couple stands under when they get married.

Kishkes: Literally means "insides". In this case it mean testicles.

Klutz: A clumsy, awkward person.

Kvetcher: A complainer.

Mazel Tov: Congratulations.

Putz: Slang for penis, more offensive than schmuck.

Schmaltz: Corny, cheesy.

Schmuck: Slang for penis, less offensive than putz.

Schmutz: Dirt.

Verklempt: Overcome with emotion.

Additional Works

Writing as Samantha Garman

The Sibby Series:
Queen of Klutz (Book 1)
Sibby Slicker (Book 2)

From Stardust to Stardust

Writing as Emma Slate

SINS Series:
Sins of a King (Book 1)
Birth of a Queen (Book 2)
Rise of a Dynasty (Book 3)
Dawn of an Empire (Book 4)

Ember Series (SINS Series Spinoff):
Ember (Book 1)
Burn (Book 2)
Ashes (Book 3)

Additional Works

Web Series:
Web of Innocence (Book 1)
Web of Deception (Book 2)

About the Author

Samantha Garman writes stories of love, laughter, and life. She is a lover of all things romance, a full-time puppy mama, and a bonafide klutz.

When she's not busy spilling things on herself, she can be found reading a book or taking photos of the wee beasties and posting them on Instagram.